P9-CCS-821

Stand in the Wind

Other books by Jean Little

MINE FOR KEEPS
A Little, Brown Canadian Prize Book
HOME FROM FAR
SPRING BEGINS IN MARCH
WHEN THE PIE WAS OPENED (Poems)
TAKE WING
ONE TO GROW ON
LOOK THROUGH MY WINDOW
KATE
FROM ANNA

Stand
in
the
Wind

by Jean Little

Pictures by Emily Arnold McCully

Harper & Row, Publishers
New York, Evanston, San Francisco, London

Chadron State College Library
Chadron, Nebraska

The lines from the songs "Open the Door," "She Moved Through the Fair," and "Little Girl See Through My Window" on pages 62, 63 and 67 are from the recording *Love Songs for Friends & Foes* (FA 2453) sung by Pete Seeger, copyright © 1956 by Folkways Records and Services Corp., and are used by permission.

STAND IN THE WIND

Text copyright © 1975 by Jean Little

Illustrations copyright © 1975 by Emily Arnold McCully

All rights reserved. No part of this book may be used or reproduced in any manner whatsoever without written permission except in the case of brief quotations embodied in critical articles and reviews. Printed in the United States of America. For information address Harper & Row, Publishers, Inc., 10 East 53rd Street, New York, N.Y. 10022. Published simultaneously in Canada by Fitzhenry & Whiteside Limited, Toronto.
Library of Congress Catalog Card Number: 73–5486

Trade Standard Book Number: 06–023903–4

Harpercrest Standard Book Number: 06-023904-2

FIRST EDITION

For
Mary Elizabeth Savage
who invited Martha into
her house and me into her heart

L 724 s

3.85

Baker & Taylor

11/3/78

Contents

1 | All Packed

Martha Winston had to sit on the suitcase to get it to shut. For once she was glad to be fifteen pounds overweight. As it was, she barely got the lid to close. Leaning over quickly, she snapped the catches into place. There! She had managed to squeeze in her sister Ellen's *Guide to Canadian Birds*. Ellen was going to be so busy entertaining the company that she wouldn't have spare time for bird-watching.

"Besides, I'll be home from camp in a week," Martha muttered.

Even though she had talked of nothing but camp for days, it still amazed her that she was really going. She looked around the room she and Ellen shared when they were here at the cottage. She had slept here every summer as far back as she could remember. It seemed strange to be planning to spend a week in July somewhere else.

But the rest of the family was leaving, too, the day after tomorrow. With guests coming, they needed the extra bedrooms in the house in town.

None of that mattered right now though. Getting

herself ready to leave for camp was the one important thing. She was positive she had forgotten something.

Of course! She jumped up and headed for the door.

Ellen, coming in to change out of her bathing suit, blocked her way.

"Where's the fire?" she asked.

"Extra flashlight batteries!" Martha cried. "I just remembered them this minute."

Ellen took her by the shoulders, turned her firmly around and pushed her back into the room.

"You do not need another thing, Martha Jane Winston," she said. "You put brand-new batteries in that flashlight just this morning. I saw you. You'll be home next Saturday, for crying out loud!"

Martha twisted free and faced the older girl.

"But what if I DO need them?" she wailed.

"You can buy them at the Camp Tuck Shop," Ellen told her calmly.

"Oh," Martha said.

Ellen edged past her, stepped over the suitcase, skirted Martha's rubber boots and halted by the chair on which she had left her clothes. Martha, feeling deflated, stood still and watched while Ellen skinned out of her bathing suit, put on shorts and a sleeveless top, hung her suit on the hook behind the door and collapsed on her bunk. Martha looked up at hers, and decided it was not worthwhile climbing up to it.

"Make more room," she told her older sister.

Ellen shifted her long legs to leave space enough for Martha to sit.

"Whew! It sure is hot," Ellen said.

"You don't look hot."

"I am boiling," Ellen retorted.

Martha mopped her own damp forehead with her shirttail, looked at her sister and sighed. Martha's short summer haircut had taken the weight of hair off the back of her neck but what was left clung stickily to her head. Ellen's, much fairer, had a bit of wave and lay loosely. Ellen's cheeks, too, were only faintly flushed in spite of the sun. Martha could see her own face in the mirror across the room. She was as red as a strawberry.

Of course, she's been swimming and I've been slaving over the packing, Martha comforted herself.

Yet thin people always looked cooler whatever they did.

Even Ellen's eyes were cooler, grey like rain clouds, while Martha's were the bright, bright blue of a clear sky in summer.

"I can't stand the thought of having to leave this nice cottage and go back to roast in town just because these people are coming," Ellen complained.

For one moment Martha thought about the visitors. Nell Swann, a college friend of her mother's, and her two daughters were coming to stay while Mr. Swann attended a convention in nearby Toronto. Mother had not seen Mrs. Swann for years, but they wrote to each other so Martha knew that the two girls were almost exactly the same ages as Ellen and herself. It was too bad the cottage did not have more bedrooms. Summers in town were awful.

But I'll be at camp for just about the whole time, Martha remembered with an inner jump for joy.

She did not answer Ellen.

"I'm sure I've forgotten something," she said instead, gazing at her stuff.

"You have not." Ellen propped herself up on one elbow so that she too could survey Martha's belongings. "Just look at it all! One sleeping bag with an extra blanket and your pillow rolled up inside it. . . ."

"It looks perfect, doesn't it?" Martha put in.

Ellen ignored that.

"Two rubber boots and one raincoat," she went on. "Maybe you should take Mother's good umbrella too."

"Don't be dumb," Martha told her.

"I seem to detect one fishing rod," Ellen said.

"Check," returned Martha.

"And a large suitcase containing . . . let me guess . . . one pair of warm pajamas, one toothbrush, one partly used tube of toothpaste, two bathing suits, towels, a couple of sweaters, blue jeans, shorts, tops, underwear, your squall jacket, some stuff to keep mosquitoes off, your drinking mug . . ." She hesitated.

"Soap in a soap dish," prompted Martha. "A plastic one with a lid."

Ellen looked at her.

"What's so remarkable about a plastic soap dish?"

"Nothing. I just never had one before."

Martha settled herself more comfortably and added, "Go on."

"What do you mean, go on?"

"Go on saying what I'm taking."

"But you've packed and repacked it all a hundred times," Ellen protested.

"I know, but I still like to hear everything in a long list like that," Martha said.

Couldn't Ellen feel the magic in the words as she said them?

Sleeping bag! Martha, in her imagination, was on a camp sleep-out. She saw the red glow of the dying fire, heard her friend Tracey laughing softly beside her and looked up into the night sky patterned with stars.

Fishing rod! Maybe she would get up at sunrise to go fishing. They had rowboats at the camp. Everything would be hushed except for the gentle creak and splash of the oars as they pulled through the water.

Flashlight! She would use it to find her way to the cabin after dark, the bobbing circle of light just ahead of her feet showing her the rocks and hollows.

And her own new soap dish! It too was special when you had always just used the soap that lay in its place on the basin in the bathroom. Martha had never been particularly fond of washing her face but at camp even that promised to be an adventure.

Then, in the middle of her daydream, Martha heard Ellen chuckle.

"What's so funny?" Martha demanded.

"You are," Ellen said. "You'd think you were off to Zanzibar or something. What's so great and marvelous about going to camp for a week? I think you're crazy in the head."

"I am not," Martha retorted. "But I'd rather go to camp any day than go to Zanzibar. Where is Zanzibar anyway?"

"Who knows?" Ellen fell back on her pillow with a sigh. "All I do know is that I wish I was going to camp with you."

Martha stared at her.

"But that one time you did go, you said you hated camp. And every time Mother's tried to talk you into going again, you've said no."

"Mother thinks I was just too young and she's probably right. I thought I'd die of homesickness," Ellen remembered. "And I hated never having time alone to do what I wanted. Though all I really wanted to do was stay in my cabin and cry. But that was six years ago. And even if it wasn't perfect, going to camp would be better than having to entertain those Swann girls for days on end. In town too, where it'll be so hot and the house will be jammed with people."

Martha counted heads. Her young brothers, Bruce and Toby, Ellen, her parents, Mrs. Swann and the two girls—that made eight people. When she came back from camp there would be nine and if Mr. Swann stayed over a night that would make it ten. Poor Ellen!

For herself, Martha would not mind if twenty people came. She liked new people. But Ellen, though she was older, never seemed to know what to say to strangers.

"It'll be okay once they get here." Martha did her best to be comforting. "I bet those girls will be really nice."

If it hadn't been for camp, she would have envied Ellen.

"Rosemary and Christine," Ellen said gloomily. "Even their names are awful."

"Maybe they'll have nicknames."

"Yeah. Rosie and Chrissy. How sweet!" Ellen jeered.

Then her lips twitched, in spite of her, and Martha grinned with relief.

"Wait till the kids in my cabin see Henrietta and

Herman," she gloated, her thoughts leaving the Swanns.

"Martha, you didn't pack those repulsive things!" Ellen cried. "Why, some of the little kids will be petrified!"

Martha opened her mouth to explain that that was the whole idea but changed her mind.

Nobody in her family, except Toby, understood her delight in practical jokes. She had no intention of taking Henrietta or Herman out of that suitcase. Henrietta was a huge hairy spider, made of rubber, but more horrible than any actual spider could be. When you twitched the thread that controlled her, her long skinny legs took jumpy little steps in the direction of your victim. Herman was a snake and also rubber—but he made other rubber snakes look like nothing. Even Toby had yelped with alarm when he had first met Herman one night, coiled on his pillow; and Toby was fond of snakes. It had cost Martha three weeks' allowance to buy Herman, but she considered him a fine investment. She had a shoe box full of other tricks, all bought with her own money, but they were more ordinary.

"Ellen. EL-LEN!" Toby's voice cannoned up the stairs.

"What is it?" Ellen called back.

"MOTHER SAYS COME AND HELP GET LUNCH RIGHT NOW!"

"Okay, okay. I'll be right down." Ellen slid her feet out around Martha and stood up.

"Thank goodness they don't have boys anyway," she said.

"They DO have boys. It's a coed camp," Martha said.

Ellen gave her a dirty look.

"I was talking about the Swanns," she said, "but all you ever think about is camp, camp, camp. Maybe something will happen to keep you home. Remember last year?"

Martha remembered.

"It wasn't my fault," she said. "I didn't know the camps filled up so fast, and I had to play at that stupid recital. I just forgot all about having the registration form. And then I couldn't find it."

"I should know. I was the one who finally did find it scrunched up in your blazer pocket. If you'd ever put things away . . ."

"Don't preach," Martha told her. "It was bad enough that I was the only one who had to stay behind. This time nothing can keep me home. Nothing!"

"Touch wood," Ellen said, turning to leave.

Martha patted the end of the bunk. Then she got up too. As she came out into the narrow hall that ran around the stairwell like the deck of a ship, she almost stepped on Bruce. He was so quiet it was hard to believe he and Toby were actually brothers, both of whom the Winstons had adopted.

Yet Ellen and I are just as different, Martha thought.

9

"Hi, Bashful," she said.

Bruce wasted no time on flippant greetings.

"Guess what I found, Marth," he said, hands behind his back.

"A lizard," guessed Martha.

He shook his head.

"A pot of gold?"

"No. Really guess."

Martha was sure she already knew but he wanted so much to surprise her. She scratched her head.

"Um . . . I don't know, Bruce. A new penny?"

Bruce, beaming, slowly extended his grubby hand, palm up.

"A wishing stone!" Martha exclaimed, doing her best to look amazed.

He had wanted one since Martha had read him a fairy tale where the hero got his heart's desire all from a wishing stone. Toby had wanted one too, but he was quickly satisfied with a small rock he picked up five minutes after he started looking. Bruce had searched carefully and long for a stone which was smooth and round and white. When he found one, he went right on looking, determined to find one for Martha too. Now Martha took the pebble from him and ran her fingers over its polished surface.

"It's even better than yours," she told him.

"Martha! Bruce! Lunch!" Mother called from the foot of the stairs.

"Coming," Martha answered. But Bruce barred her way.

"Martha, maybe I'd better keep the stone for you until you're ready to wish," he said. "It's awfully easy to say something without thinking and then everything you touch turns to gold or you have a pudding on the end of your nose or something."

"How about you?" Martha said, trying not to laugh.

"I'll be very careful," Bruce assured her, and took back the stone.

"Let's go." Suddenly starving, Martha ran slam-bang down the stairs, jumping the last three, sailed across the living room and landed on her chair with a crash.

"Martha, those stairs are dangerous," Mother scolded. "Someday you're going to come flying down like that and break your neck."

"Not me," Martha said. "Hey, I'm all packed to go."

Her mother laughed at her.

"You've been packed for a week," she said. "You just can't stop rearranging things. Toby, will you ask the blessing, please?"

"God is great and God is good. Let us thank Him for this food. Amen. I want a peanut-butter sand-wich," Toby said in a breathless rush.

"Not till you've finished your soup," Mrs. Win-ston said. "And eaten some carrot sticks."

Toby went at his soup as though he had had no nourishment for a week. Bruce bent forward and blew gently on his.

"It's cool enough to eat now, Bruce, if you start from the edge," Mother said.

"I like it COLD," Bruce answered quietly but firmly.

Toby spooned in his last mouthful and grabbed three carrot sticks.

"Rabbit food!" he scoffed, chomping into them like a beaver demolishing a tree trunk.

Bruce took one in his left hand. He nibbled at it with his front teeth. Martha, noticing, knew he was playing he was a rabbit.

"Bruce," Mother said suddenly as he picked up his spoon again, "what's wrong with your right hand?"

"I'm holding something in it," Bruce said.

"Well, put it down and eat properly. You're going to spill your soup that way."

Bruce turned a troubled face to Martha.

That crazy wishing stone!

"Give it here," Martha said quickly. "I've thought of one."

Bruce handed her the smooth white pebble and watched to make sure she wished the way she should. Martha closed her eyes, rubbed the wishing stone three times, clutched it tightly and thought.

I wish the camp I'm going to will be the most fun I've ever had in my whole entire life.

Toby, swinging around to watch too, knocked over his milk. His mother snatched up paper napkins and tried to check the spreading white lake.

"Quick, Martha. Get the dishcloth," she ordered.

Martha ran. Rounding the corner into the kitchen, she skidded on the floor. As she slipped, she grabbed for the counter to break her fall but the wishing stone was still in her hand. Instinctively she threw out her other arm.

Crash!

"Martha, what happened? Are you all right?" Mrs. Winston cried.

"Hurry," yelled Toby. "The milk's running into my shoe!"

Martha did not answer. She sat where she had fallen, her teeth clenched, her left arm cradled awkwardly against her.

"Oh, Martha, what now?" Mother was kneeling beside her.

"My arm." Martha tried not to cry. "It hurts."

Her mother reached out, felt Martha flinch and drew back her hand. She stood up then and turned to Ellen, who was watching from the door.

"Dr. Hill's at his cottage. Call and ask him to come."

Ellen stared down at Martha, still huddled on the floor.

"What's the matter with her?" she asked.

"I'm not sure," Caroline Winston said, "but I think she's just broken her arm."

2 | Why Couldn't We?

Martha stumbled wearily up the path to the cottage. Ellen had heard the car stop. She met them at the back door. Her eyes widened as she caught sight of the sling.

"You really DID break it then!" she exclaimed.

Martha nodded. For one proud moment she forgot the misery of the bumpy ride into town, the long wait at the hospital, the pain, the worry and the heat. Then she collapsed into the nearest chair and let Mother do any talking that needed doing.

"It isn't a bad break," Mother explained. "She's just cracked her radius. Right here," she went on, pointing out the exact spot on Ellen's elbow. "She doesn't need a cast and she'll only have to have it in a sling for a couple of weeks, though it'll take longer than that to heal completely."

Ellen looked at Martha and lowered her voice.

"Can she still go tomorrow?"

"The doctor says she can if the camp will take her," Mother said. "I'll call and check. Did the boys go to bed without any trouble?"

14

"Just the usual," Ellen said. "Toby said he really thought you'd want him to wait up for you."

"Trust Toby." Mother smiled. "You take Martha up and help her undress. She's practically asleep on her feet. Her arm hurts if she tries to straighten it out."

Martha roused.

"Are you going to phone the camp right now?" she asked.

"In about two minutes. I promise I'll come up and report the instant I'm finished."

"Okay," Martha agreed.

She tried to get up. She had chosen a low soft chair without arms. She struggled and sank back, surprised.

"I'm stuck here," she said.

Ellen took hold of her right hand and tugged her up.

"Come on," she said, steering her sister toward the stairs.

"I remember undressing you when you were little," she said minutes later as she eased Martha's blouse off.

"What was I like?" Martha mumbled.

She felt sleep closing in around her like a fog. She shook her head to clear it and her arm jerked too.

"Ouch!" she said, waking up.

"You were bratty," Ellen said. "Kind of cute though. Here are your pajama pants."

"I can put them on myself," Martha said.

It was harder than she had thought it would be. Once she let go of them for a second while she got a better grip; they slid to her ankles.

Brushing her teeth was easy, though Ellen put the toothpaste on the brush for her. Helping her do things was going to keep Tracey busy when they got to camp.

"Can you make it up to your bunk?" Ellen asked.

Martha looked up and knew she couldn't. She should have kept the ladder, but she had never used it and it got in Ellen's way.

"You can sleep in my bed," Ellen said. "I'll get your pillow."

Martha climbed in and lay down. It was wonderful to lie still and know you could stay.

"Ellen," she said drowsily.

Ellen did not answer. Martha looked for her and saw Mother standing in the doorway.

"What did they say?" Ellen spoke into the silence.

"They said no," Mother answered. Her words seemed to reach Martha from far away, but she could not stop herself hearing them. "They said they couldn't take the responsibility. Their insurance would not cover her if there were complications."

"But, Mother, the doctor . . ." Ellen began.

"I told them what the doctor said. I told them nothing would go wrong. I promised we would take

16

full responsibility. I said . . . Well, what does it matter what I said? They wouldn't listen. Ellen, don't keep going over it. You'll only make things harder."

Mother seated herself beside Martha on the lower bunk. She stretched out a hand and brushed Martha's hair back.

"I'm sorry, Martha," she said. "You've had a rough day. The doctor gave me something to help you sleep tonight. How does your arm feel?"

Martha could not answer. Tears were running down her cheeks. Mother went and came back with cold water and a pill. She propped Martha up. As she held the glass for her, she raised her head and listened.

"There's your father, Ellen," she said. "Go and tell him what's happened. I couldn't reach him when we were in town. Make sure he gets some supper."

Ellen started for the door.

"He'll want to come up," she said softly.

"Tell him not tonight," Mother answered. "She's worn out and she's had that pill."

"Okay," Ellen said. She paused, one hand on the knob, and looked down at her sister.

"I think it's the meanest thing I ever heard of," she declared.

"Turn out the light, would you, dear?" Mother requested.

Suddenly the small room was dark. Martha wept on.

"Shhh," Mother said. "Take long easy breaths. That's it. Now try to sleep."

"I can't," gulped Martha.

"Shhh," Mother said again, and she began to sing.

The hurt gripping Martha let go a little as she listened to the old lullaby which she had known ever since she could remember. She was so tired. Before the song was finished, she was asleep.

At breakfast the next morning everybody was so kind that Martha wanted to scream. Even when her father greeted her with a careful hug, she felt cranky as a bear.

"Don't," she said, pulling away.

He looked surprised but he just said, "I'm sorry this happened, Martha."

"I know," Martha muttered, hanging her head.

Next thing she knew, Ellen was pouring her milk. Mother made her toast and spread it with butter and honey. When she dropped her napkin, Bruce dove so quickly to retrieve it for her that their heads almost bumped. Even Toby watched her with saucer eyes as though she were a visiting princess.

"Thank you," Martha had to say. Over and over and over. Long before they were finished eating, she was dying to be really rude to somebody, anybody.

Her father studied her unhappy face.

18

"Your arm doesn't hurt, does it, Martha?" he asked.

"No. It's fine," she told him.

Had they forgotten about camp? Nobody had even mentioned it. Then she looked around from face to face and she knew that her whole family remembered. That was why they were being so terribly kind.

As if getting your toast buttered would make up for having to stay home from camp!

She jammed her last bite in and spoke with her mouth full.

"I'm going out," she announced, shoving her chair back.

Nobody said anything for an instant. Then Ellen asked meekly, "Would you like me to come with you?"

"No," Martha flung at her.

She bolted out of the room and escaped. Once on the beach, she hesitated.

"You cut that out right now, Stanley Brownley, or I'll tell," shrilled a child's voice.

Martha grinned, her grouchiness lifting. Andrea Brownley was squealing threats at her big brother just as she did every day. Martha started toward them. They would be terribly impressed by her sling. Then she stopped, turned around and headed in the opposite direction.

19

She would show them later. Now she wanted to be by herself.

The water drew her like a magnet. For a moment, she played with it, trying to wade with one foot while she kept the other out of reach on the packed wet sand at the edge of the lake. She leaped out of the way of one wave, barely managed to evade the second but was fairly caught by the third. She did not mind. She loved being in the water. She waded on, delighting in the pull of the undertow, gentle on this windless day, as it sucked the sand out from under her bare feet only to send it swirling back again in the next oncoming wave.

Suddenly she thought of her worried family.

"They probably think I'm bawling," she said aloud.

For an instant she was dangerously close to it, but she herself drove the threatening tears away.

"Fifteen men on a dead man's chest," she chanted, booming out the words in her deepest voice.

And she pranced a few steps like a circus horse, jerking her knees high and tossing her head. Water churned around her and splashed up onto her shorts. She held her arm braced firmly against her so it would not hurt.

She was making so much noise she almost missed hearing Ellen.

"Mar-tha! MARTHA!"

"What?" she shouted in return, looking back until

she spotted her sister standing in front of the cottage.

"Come on back. You have to pack!"

For a split second, Martha's heart leaped. Had the people at the camp changed their minds? Was she going to be able to go after all?

Then she remembered that this afternoon the Winstons were moving back to town so they would be there when the visitors arrived. The sun still shone but, to Martha, it seemed as though someone had yanked down a dark blind, hiding the brightness of the morning.

"I'm already packed," she shouted in Ellen's direction.

Not waiting for an answer, she splashed on through the water. But the fun had gone out of wading.

What else was there? She looked up and down the stretch of sand.

The swings!

Maybe wading and swinging were babyish but she liked both. She marched toward the distant swings. As she drew nearer, she saw there was someone already there. A second later, she recognized Bruce. She hesitated. He had his back to her. Then she took pity on him.

He was trying to swing by himself, but he had never learned how to pump properly. She saw him straining his thin arms, struggling to make the swing

21

go, but he didn't know what to do with the rest of his body. In spite of his efforts, the swing only rocked in place.

Martha said nothing till she was close enough to touch him.

"Relax," she said then. "I'll start you off."

Bruce flashed a startled look over his shoulder. She put all her strength into her right hand and pushed squarely in the middle of his back. Three more pushes and he was swooping up into the air like a bird.

"Thanks, Marth," he shouted as he flew back toward her.

"It's my pleasure," Martha said.

She settled herself on the swing next to his. Then, for the first time, she realized that without the use of both hands, she was also unable to swing properly.

What a morning!

She decided to push Bruce some more. She might as well. There was nothing better to do.

"That's enough, Martha," Bruce said ten minutes later. He stared across at her as she sank back down on her swing. "You look like a wounded hero," he said.

Martha made a face.

"I'd rather look like my ordinary self and go to camp," she retorted.

Saying it, right out loud, made her feel better. She smiled reassuringly at the small boy.

Bruce looked away from her. His gaze traveled the

length of the sunny beach, skimmed the bright water and took in the huge blueness of the sky.

"I just wish we could stay out here and not have to go to town," he said.

Martha opened her mouth to agree.

"Well, I'm not going with you, of course," she found herself saying. "I AM staying here."

Bruce twisted sideways so that he faced her. His eyes were wide with astonishment. Then they narrowed. She kept her face straight with difficulty.

"All by yourself?" Bruce asked.

Martha decided he would never believe her unless she changed her story a bit.

"Of course not. Don't be so silly. Ellen's staying too," she told him. She dug into the sand with her toes and waited to see what he would say next.

"You're fooling," he said doubtfully. Then when she shook her head, he came up with a new challenge.

"Who'll look after you?"

"We can take care of ourselves," Martha said, stung by his lack of faith in his sisters. At that point, her imagination ran away with her. "We're even going to have a camp here, so there," she said.

"Two people can't have a camp." Bruce was positive now.

"Ellen and I can," Martha retorted. She went on giddily, "Ellen will get us up by blowing a whistle and then we'll go for Morning Dip."

"You can't go in swimming with a broken arm."

23

"I can so if I keep my arm in the sling. The doctor said it was okay. Even if I couldn't, somebody has to watch when Ellen swims."

Bruce nodded. He knew you couldn't swim alone without a lifeguard.

"And we'll have singsongs . . ."

"Just the two of you?"

"Why not? You sing lots of times all by yourself."

Martha sounded so definite and her answers made sense.

"And we'll do a Craft," she dreamed on.

"What Craft?" Bruce was growing really interested.

Martha wished he would stop interrupting her with tricky questions.

"We haven't decided yet," she said loftily. "But boy, are we ever going to have fun!"

Bruce slid off his swing.

"I'm going to ask Mother if Toby and I can stay too," he cried, his face ablaze with excitement.

He raced away before she could stop him. Martha burst out laughing. Then, wanting to save him disappointment, she thought fast and called after him, "Bruce, it's a girls' camp!"

He sped on, obviously not hearing.

They'll think he's lost his marbles, Martha thought, and laughed again. She put off going home, though. She did not want to face Bruce till he had had time to forgive her for fooling him.

Heading away from home, she went for a long walk. At noon she was a couple of miles from the cottage. Suddenly very hungry, she started back. It was hard to hurry in the sand. She cut up behind the cottages and continued by the back lane. A car came toward her. She stepped off into the grass to let it pass.

"Hey, Martha!" a voice yelled.

It was the Winstons' car. Toby screamed his greeting as they swept past. Mother waved. But they did not stop.

Martha stepped back onto the gravel and kept going. They had not even slowed down. She knew she was late. But had they deserted her?

"Martha!"

Ellen burst out of the cottage and Martha, though she had really been sure they would never have left her, still drew a breath of relief.

"I saw the car," she said. "Where . . . ?"

"The Swanns have come." Ellen could hardly get the words out fast enough. "Mrs. Redding saw them ringing our doorbell and she phoned. They got here a day early for some reason. So the family went to meet them."

"Is Mother mad at me for being late?" Martha asked.

Ellen stared at her. Then she grinned.

"Nobody's mad at you. Personally I think you are marvelous. The way you rescued us was like magic!"

"Me?" Martha looked as bewildered as she felt. Ellen calmed down slightly.

"Bruce told us," she explained. "About your great idea—how you and I could stay here by ourselves. Mother told him you were teasing. But then I said, 'Why couldn't we?' Mother said, 'Because of the Swanns, for one thing.' I was stumped for a second but I felt desperate. I didn't plan what to say. The words just came."

"What words?" Martha demanded, trying to bring Ellen to the point.

"I said, 'Why not bring the girls out here and let us stay by ourselves and you can entertain Mrs. Swann in town?' Mother wasn't listening, really, but Dad spoke right up. 'That's a good suggestion, Ellen,' he said. Then he helped persuade her. Finally I said . . ."

Ellen stopped suddenly and looked away. Her face reddened.

"What?" Martha prodded.

"It doesn't matter," Ellen started. Then her own honesty made her tell. "I said it would help you not to mind missing camp so much and stuff like that. And Mother gave in if Mrs. Swann agrees. I don't see why she shouldn't. I'm a very responsible girl."

"Rosie and Chrissy and us," mused Martha.

But she, like Ellen, felt the stir of excitement that comes on the brink of a big adventure.

"They'll get here sometime after supper," Ellen said.

Suddenly she gave Martha a scared look. Martha knew how she felt. They did not know these girls! What would the four of them do?

All this, she thought in amazement, because I teased Bruce.

Then she remembered everything she had told him.

"We really can have a camp," she said.

"Martha, a camp wouldn't work with just four people," Ellen broke in quickly. "But we will be able to stay at the beach instead of sweltering in town. That's better than nothing, isn't it?"

Martha smiled.

Camp Better-Than-Nothing, a voice inside her head said.

It sounded fine. Just fine!

3 | The Swanns

Another car! Martha tensed, leaning close to the window, but the car hummed past.

Soon. Maybe the very next one.

Waiting, she relaxed slightly. She turned her head and watched Ellen, sitting under a reading lamp, intent on a book. Ellen appeared calm, as though she felt no wheeling butterflies inside.

But she hasn't turned a page in ages, Martha noted.

Suddenly she swept her gaze around the cottage itself. Would the Swanns like it? Or would they think it small and ordinary? Now darkness was falling, the view was not waiting to catch your breath.

It's perfect, Martha thought defiantly.

But it really wasn't very big. She was sitting in the sun porch. The back door opened into it, beside the chair where she was perched, and, opposite her, doors led into the tiny kitchen on her left and the living room-dining room on her right. The dining part came first. It was narrower. And then the roomy living room with its tall French doors looking out over sand, water and sky. Martha had always liked the fact that you could see right through the cottage from front to back and beyond if you were in the right place. Right now, past Ellen reading, she glimpsed the faint streaks of amber left by the sunset in the twilight sky.

Upstairs seemed downright skimpy, all at once, although there was plenty of room for the Winstons. There were three bedrooms strung out along the narrow slice of hall and a box of a bathroom at the head of the stairs.

Not even a bathtub, thought Martha.

Then she grinned. Never before had she missed having a bathtub.

"Martha," Ellen said sharply.

Then Martha too heard the oncoming car. She got up on her knees and pressed her nose against the glass.

"Yes," she yelped, leaping back, "it's them. They're stopping."

She had dodged back so she would not be spotted but she still could watch the people climbing out of the car. They were pale blurs in the dusk. But in a moment, they would be real. They had come to stay.

Martha shot across the room and stood as close to her big sister as she could get.

"I'm scared!" Her words were a squeak of panic.

29

"Shut up," Ellen told her.

The pair of them waited frozen in their places. They heard the trunk lid creak up and bang back down. Voices murmured words they could not catch. Then one phrase of Mother's sounded out.

". . . dying to meet them. . . ."

Feet were nearing, scratching on the walk.

Martha could not stand it. She felt trapped.

"They'll catch us," she said wildly.

Ellen, as though she knew exactly what she was doing, reached up in one swift motion and switched off the single light.

Darkness hid them. They were safe.

The next instant, both girls realized how ridiculous they would look caught sitting there in the dark. Ellen groped desperately for the light switch she had found so easily a second before. Martha, trying to help, got in her way.

Too soon, Mother opened the cottage door. She was in the sun porch. They could hear every word she said.

"Goodness, it's dark. I thought I saw a light when we were driving up but the girls must be upstairs. Stay there or you'll be tripping over each other."

Still talking, she came into the dining room and flicked the wall switch. Her daughters, right in front of her, blinked at the suddenness of the light. There was a short astonished silence.

"Why, girls," Mother exclaimed at last. Then she

waited. Martha waited too, hoping Ellen would try to explain. Ellen just sat.

Well, somebody had to do something!

Martha laughed. It was a brave act, though nobody except Ellen appreciated that.

"We wanted to scare you," Martha said, relying on her past reputation to make Mother believe her. Mother did.

"Really, Martha," she began, her blue eyes sparking with anger. Then she remembered the guests and left her lecture till later.

The Swanns had followed her into the sun porch as soon as the light came on. Martha could not see them yet but she knew they must have heard.

Then Mrs. Swann swept in and Martha forgot her embarrassment.

"Here's that naughty old broken arm we've been hearing about," Nell Swann cried, flashing a huge smile at Martha. "You poor, poor baby!"

"It's okay," Martha growled.

Poor, poor baby! What kind of talk was that?

And Mrs. Swann looked all wrong. Martha had seen her mother and her mother's college friends in old pictures. None of those laughing girls in the old-fashioned clothes had looked the least bit like Mrs. Swann. Mother still looked like the same person—only now she was grown-up and somehow more real. Mrs. Swann, to Martha, in that first instant, looked totally unreal.

"As though she was standing in front of a TV camera every minute," Martha tried to explain to Ellen afterward.

Mrs. Swann had a pile of flaming red curls, stylish glasses, makeup that looked like it did on TV and a dress . . . !

Mother would never wear something like that to a cottage. Martha dismissed the dress. She knew what she thought of Mrs. Swann, and none of it was good.

"And this must be Ellen!" Mrs. Swann bubbled on, making bad worse. "To think I still have your baby picture and now you're the big grown-up girl who's going to look after my two innocent babes! I hope you can cook. Rosemary and Christine have never shown the slightest wish to learn."

"I'm not so great at it either." Ellen sounded as gruff as Martha. "But I guess we'll survive."

"Nell, that's hardly fair," a man said. "Rosemary and Kit haven't had a chance."

Martha craned her neck, trying to see around Mrs. Swann, but the woman stood squarely in front of her. She did turn though and call her older daughter forward to share the limelight.

"This is my Rosemary." The mother's voice dripped with pride and Martha saw why right away. Rosemary Swann was a second edition of her mother. No curls but the same fiery red hair, long, silken smooth and straight. Nobody would ever call her "Carrots" either; it was too golden a red for that. She wore less makeup than her mother. Even Ellen used makeup sometimes, but never blue-green eye shadow at the beach! Rosemary wore no glasses. Her eyes were greenish and cold. They flicked over Martha, took in Ellen briefly and then looked somewhere in between them.

Poor, poor baby! Do we hurt your naughty itty-bitty eyes? Martha crooned at her, inside her head.

She did not need to see Rosemary's clothes—What Teens Are Wearing These Fun Days in the Sun!—nor listen to her cool voice when she said "Hello there," to know that Rosemary Swann was not going to fit into any camp Martha could imagine.

Martha glanced at Ellen; she looked petrified. Rosie was not a kindred spirit.

Then, just as though Mother had spoken the words aloud across the room, Martha heard, "Don't jump to conclusions, Martha. Give her a fair chance."

Okay. She'd been wrong before. But Martha was almost one hundred per cent sure Rosemary would not improve no matter how many chances she got.

What about Christine though? If Mrs. Swann ever hushed . . .

". . . such a marvelous time out here in this cozy wee place! How I envy you all!" Mrs. Swann was still at it. Then, as if Martha's thoughts had secret power, she said, "But you haven't met my baby yet, though she's really more her Daddy's girl in lots of ways. Come here, Christine. Don't hang back in the shadows."

"Easy, Kit," Martha heard Mr. Swann say.

Christine stepped forward. Martha took one look and gasped. Christine Swann looked all of six years old!

She was wearing a pale-blue dress with a very full skirt and a round white collar. There were tiny white flowers embroidered on the yoke. She also had on snowy-white sandals, completely unscuffed.

All she needs is a sash around her middle, a bow in her hair and a lollipop! Martha thought.

But Christine's sandy hair was held back by a plain silver hair clip exactly like those Martha wore in winter when her own hair was long enough.

"Hi," Martha blurted, remembering her manners a bit late.

Christine said "Hello" back, but she had her head ducked down so far Martha could hardly hear her.

"She's a wee bit bashful, I'm afraid, but we're working on that, aren't we, sweetheart?" her mother said, putting her arm around her daughter and giving her an encouraging squeeze. The girl made no answer but, as soon as she could, she freed herself and moved quickly back to stand beside her father. Mrs. Swann had shifted now, turning to say some-

34

thing to Mother, so Martha saw Mr. Swann put his hand lightly on Christine's shoulder. She raised her head and Martha caught the quick smile father and daughter exchanged.

It wasn't a baby smile. Maybe Chrissy wasn't all bad.

"Kit's not bashful; she just knows when to talk," her father said.

Martha's mother broke in then, telling them all to sit down and asking Ellen whether she had managed to get everything done on the list Caroline Winston had left her. Remembering, Martha sighed. She hated housework and they had had to make beds, get out fresh towels, clean up generally—with special attention to the chaos in Toby and Bruce's room. Martha had done her best to get out of helping because of her broken arm but Ellen had found dozens of one-handed jobs for her to do.

"Everything's ready," Ellen reported.

"Well, I brought some food. Come to the kitchen and I'll show you," Mother said. Then, looking back at the waiting faces, she suddenly suggested, "When I've shown her, let's go. It'll be easier for the girls to settle in by themselves and we have to get back to town. Mrs. Redding's watching Bruce and Toby, but she wants to be home by ten. We can phone here tomorrow and find out if there are any problems. And you girls, if you need us, phone right away. It doesn't take that long to get here."

"Well, if you think that's best . . ." Mrs. Swann looked unsure.

She probably knows Christine'll be lonesome without her, Martha scoffed to herself.

Then she swallowed. At the thought of Mother leaving, she felt close to crying herself.

"I think that's a fine idea," Mr. Swann said, getting to his feet.

"Where's Dad?" Martha said, realizing belatedly that he was missing.

Mother and Ellen were still in the kitchen. Mrs. Swann said vaguely, "At some sort of meeting."

"City Council," Mr. Swann said, giving Martha a smile. Martha smiled back. So far, he was far and away her favorite among the Swanns. With him about to desert her, Christine was positively hunched over, staring at the floor. Rosemary gazed steadily into space and looked bored to her fingertips.

And Ellen, coming back from the kitchen, stopped in her tracks at the sight of them all and, when she started up again, moved like a sleepwalker.

Help! Martha thought. Help, help, HELP!!

But ten minutes later, the adults were gone.

The intense silence which fell upon the four girls the moment the car drove off seemed to go on forever. Nobody knew what to say, what to do or where to look. Even Rosemary, though still bored, seemed distinctly uncomfortable.

Then Martha made herself snap out of it. After

all, they could not just stand there like dummies for the next eight days.

"Hey, no grown-ups!" she announced brightly.

Ellen looked at her younger sister the way someone who is drowning looks at someone standing safely on shore.

"So what do we do now?" she asked in a thin voice.

"We show them around, I guess," Martha said sensibly. "It won't take too long. We all know this cozy wee place isn't Buckingham Palace."

Rosemary smiled, but it was a mechanical smile. Martha saw at once that she was the only one of the three of them who had caught Martha's use of Mrs. Swann's words.

Suddenly Martha Winston knew she was tired out. Her arm ached. All day long she had fought off thoughts of Tracey and the others leaving for camp, but now she knew that that was where Tracey was, right this minute, with her sleeping bag and her flashlight and probably even her soap in a plastic soap dish.

Martha laughed to keep from crying. It was a queer croaky laugh but it helped her get back the strength she needed. Let them fall apart and act like a bunch of goons if they chose. She wasn't going to.

"You get a great view of the lake through those glass doors in the daytime," she told the visitors, just as though the visitors were interested. "And there's a beautiful beach. Can you swim?"

"I teach swimming at the Y," Rosemary said.
Martha waited but Christine volunteered nothing. Probably still struggling to master the dog paddle!

"Well, that's good," Martha said. "It's shallow, but if you wade out far enough, it gets deep. We go swimming every day."

"Where's the TV?" Rosemary asked. "Do you get good reception away out here?"

Ignoring Martha, Rosemary aimed her question straight at Ellen. Martha shut her lips tightly. She wished Ellen the best of luck.

"We don't have a television at the cottage." Ellen's voice faltered over these words as though she was confessing to a major crime. "We like to read and stuff. The cottage is too small if someone has TV on. It's good for Toby and Bruce too. They can actually get off *Sesame Street* and just play wherever they please."

"I took a course in Childhood Education last term," Rosemary said, not smiling. "My teacher said *Sesame Street* stimulated children to use their imaginations."

"Bruce and Toby don't need to be stimulated; they need to be calmed down," Martha said. "And they have the alphabet right down pat."

"Martha," Ellen warned. Everything was going wrong and Martha wasn't helping. The look in Ellen's eyes cried for help. Martha did her best.

"We have fun here really," she said. "You'll like it once you're used to it. Why don't you come and see where you sleep and stuff?"

"But what do you DO?" Rosemary's voice had a frantic note in it. "Do you have a stereo?"

"We have a record player but it's a portable one. The good one's in town. And of course we have some records here but they're mostly family stuff. My records are at home." Ellen sounded miserable.

"We read a lot," Martha said, backing Ellen up. The expression on Rosemary's face would scare anybody. "And we go on walks and swimming, naturally. Dad paints when he has time. We play games. . . ."

Her voice trailed off. Days at the cottage had always seemed full of things to do, lovely summer-holiday things, but suddenly they sounded long and dull.

"What do you read?" Rosemary glanced around; there was not a book in sight.

Since each bedroom had lots of bookcase space, the shelves downstairs held pieces of driftwood, something complicated Bruce had made with Lego, a collection of rocks the boys had found—all sorts of odds and ends that had meaning for the Winstons, but nothing to read.

"Books," Ellen said. "They're upstairs."

Martha's tiredness swamped her again and she struck out at Rosemary before she could stop herself.

40

"I'm sorry but we don't have any junky nurse books or romances in the entire cottage."

"Rosemary doesn't read junk," Christine said.

It was as though the wall had spoken. Yet though Christine's voice was faint, Martha heard the hurt in it and was ashamed.

Then Rosemary did the first ordinary human thing she had done since they arrived. She yawned so widely her jaws cracked—and she forgot to cover her mouth. She went pink.

"We got up about dawn this morning," she said. "Dad has this thing about being out on the road before anybody else in the world has so much as stirred. I know it's awful but I'd really like to go to bed. I feel beat."

Martha immediately smiled at her, seeing not the mean Rosemary she had been half fighting with but the tired one who yawned just the way Martha yearned to and now did.

"I'm sleepy too, Ellen," she said. "Let's take them up right now."

Finally Ellen took charge. If Rosemary was like Mrs. Swann, Ellen was like Mother, Martha decided, listening to her start them moving. About to lead the way to the stairs, she asked if she or Martha could carry anything.

"We can manage," Rosemary said. "Pick up your feet, Christine."

Ellen going first, they climbed the narrow stairs

single file. When Martha reached the top, she gestured to the first bedroom door across from the stair head.

"This is ours," she told Christine Swann.

It was really Bruce and Toby's room but they had decided Rosemary should have their parents' room, Ellen stay where she was and Christine and Martha share.

I should have stuck with Ellen, Martha moaned to herself. I thought it would be more like camp with someone my age but . . .

"Which bed do you want, Christine?" she asked.

The other girl looked from one to the other in a daze.

"It doesn't matter," she said.

"Well, take that one then," said Martha. "And here's a place for your suitcase."

She paused to watch Christine lay her suitcase on the stand; then she blurted, "Hey, do you have a nickname? I mean, Christine sounds so formal or something. If you don't, forget it. Christine's okay, just fine."

Why can't I keep my big mouth shut? Martha wondered as she heard herself begin to babble.

"You can call me Kit," Christine said. "Dad always does."

"Kit," Martha said, trying it out. "That's neat, though it sounds more like a boy's name."

"Dad wanted a boy," Kit answered. Then, making

her longest speech to date, she said, "But he claims he wouldn't trade me for a million boys."

Martha thought of a million Tobys. Her brain reeled.

Then Rosemary's voice sounded down the hall. "Oh, how lovely!"

"It must be the moon's up," Martha explained to Kit. "Rosemary gets the full view from her window but if you kneel on my bed and look through that small window, you'll get a glimpse."

Kit did as she was bidden and caught her breath in wonder. Martha felt pleased with the cottage for showing off.

Then Rosemary spoke again. She must be talking to Ellen.

"Maybe it won't be so terrible after all," Rosemary Swann said.

Martha heard Ellen's shocked response. "You mean you didn't want to come?"

"I had other plans, that's all. It'll be okay though. I mean, it's only for a little over a week. We'll survive even if we are stranded at the end of nowhere." Rosemary suddenly seemed to realize how rude she was being. "I'm sure it will be very nice," she tacked on.

"Yeah. Well, call if you want anything. See you in the morning," Ellen said.

Martha heard her go into her own room and shut the door with a small bang.

She's wishing we were in town, Martha thought. Me too!

"What did Rosemary mean about having 'other plans'?" she asked Kit's back.

For a moment, she thought Kit was not going to answer. Then, without turning, she said, "Nancy Elliot asked her to come to their place in Maine during summer vacation."

Martha wished Kit would stop looking out the window and talk to her properly. Yet Kit did seem a bit less tongue-tied this way.

"Why wouldn't your mother let her go?" Martha asked.

"Oh, Rosemary talked Mother into it. But Dad said no."

Martha sighed. She wanted to know the whole story but getting information out of Kit was like pulling teeth. You only got one fact at a time.

"What's the matter with this Nancy?" Martha persisted.

Kit squirmed a little, then half turned but still did not look at Martha. She examined the quilt she knelt on instead, running one finger over a blue velvet square.

"Dad says she's too old for Rosemary."

Martha blinked in surprise.

Kit, not seeing, went on. "And her parents go off and leave them alone too much."

"But they've left us alone!" Martha said.

At that, Kit did look at her. Then her glance swept the small warm room, taking in the little boys' paintings taped to the wall, the bright quilts Mother had made, the bare rafters.

"Oh, this is nothing like the Elliots'," she said and stopped.

"What's it like there?" Martha tried.

Kit did not answer. It was as though she had caught herself coming through a door, suddenly realized she was in the wrong place and backed up, closing the door between herself and Martha and turning the key in the lock. Martha wanted to know more but she could tell by the set of Kit's shoulders that for now Kit had said all she was going to about Rosemary and the Elliots.

Sitting there, trying to think of how to break the silence, Martha felt an unexpected pang of sympathy for Rosemary Swann. Martha, too, had had other plans. In spite of herself, she thought of camp again. Maybe the kids would have gone to their cabins by now. Tracey was probably beginning to make new friends.

"Nuts!" Martha muttered and pulled her thoughts back to Kit. She was pretty sure that she and Kit would never become friends. But somehow she had to learn something about the other girl. If Kit, as well as Rosemary, definitely did not want to be here,

Mother would understand and come to their rescue. Kit now sat facing her, her feet dangling over the edge of the bed, her gaze fixed on the floor.

"Kit," Martha said.

"Yes," Kit answered, not moving.

Exasperated with her, Martha took a deep breath and plunged on.

"Did you want to come here?"

Kit's head came up. The sudden dazzle of joy on her face caught Martha completely off guard.

"I prayed to come," Kit Swann said. "It's like a miracle, really. It gets me out of two whole weeks at camp!"

4 | Bad Night and Bad Morning

"Oh," Martha said.

Now she was the one with nothing to say. Kit must be right out of her mind. Martha tried to keep her face blank but Kit must have caught the shock in the brown eyes staring at her. The light went out of her face.

"I d-don't like camp," she said. "Mother makes me go. She says it's . . . it's good for me."

"Oh," Martha said again. Then, "I see."

She had to stop saying "Oh" over and over again like a talking doll. She certainly did not want to talk about camp though.

"Excuse me a minute," she said. "I forgot to ask Ellen something. I'll be right back."

She burst in upon Ellen without knocking. Ellen had not started to undress. She was just sitting on her bed, doing nothing. As their eyes met, Martha knew Ellen felt exactly the way she did herself. She shut the door behind her.

"Ellen, what are we going to do?" she half whispered.

"I don't know," Ellen said. "Rosemary makes me feel as though I belong in kindergarten."

"How old is she anyway?" Martha asked. "I'm sure Mother said they were the same ages as we are but Rosemary looks nineteen or twenty."

"She is almost one whole year younger than I am," Ellen stated. Then she sighed. "But I know what you mean. She's sophisticated."

"I don't like her," Martha said, forgetting about the second chance she was going to give Rosemary. "And Kit's such a baby!"

"She's older than you, though," Ellen said. "Three months. I asked Mother their exact ages when we were out in the kitchen. Listen, Marth, you'd better go back. Rosemary can take care of herself all right, but Christine . . ."

"I know. I'll go in a second. But first let me tell you what she told me about Rosemary."

There was not much to tell but Ellen was as interested as Martha had been. Martha almost went on to tell her what Kit had said about camp. Then, not wanting Ellen's pity, she left it out.

"Tough," Ellen said when Martha had finished. She obviously felt far too sorry for herself to have any sympathy to waste on Rosemary. "Keep trying to think of some way out, Martha."

"I'm thinking every minute," Martha said, reaching for the doorknob. "Good night."

48

"I'll stop in on my way to the bathroom," Ellen offered.

"Thanks," Martha said, and went back to Kit.

Kit had not moved. She looked as though she had been crying. Her hands were scrunched together in a tight little ball in her lap. Martha tried to think of something helpful to say and gave up.

"Let's go to bed," she said instead. "You must be tired. I am."

Not waiting for Kit not to answer, she began struggling out of her clothes. She was clumsy and she felt self-conscious but she managed everything without having to ask for help. Soon Kit, too, started to undress. In a moment, Martha saw her straining to reach the buttons that did up the back of the baby-blue dress.

"I'll do the middle ones," Martha said, moving toward her.

Kit bent her arms as far as she could and undid the last one.

"Never mind," she said. "I did them myself."

She sounds just like I feel, Martha thought.

Then she saw Kit had on a slip with a wide ruffly lace border. As though she had come to a birthday party instead of a summer cottage. Martha fought down an attack of giggles.

Passing Kit's open suitcase, she was relieved to see ordinary shorts, tops and a pair of jeans. Glad the day was almost over, she climbed into bed and pulled the covers up to her chin.

"Are you two okay?" Ellen asked from the doorway.

Martha grinned at her. Ellen was a neat sister. Both of them pretended they did not see Kit scrambling modestly into a shortie nightgown.

"We're fine," Martha told Ellen.

"I'm sorry I forgot about your arm," Ellen said. "Does it ache?"

"Not really. And I managed fine by myself," Martha answered.

At that, she remembered how she had thought Tracey would help her at camp. A great longing to be there with her friends swept over her. In the same instant, she remembered how happy Kit was to "get out of" camp. She swallowed hard and closed her eyes tight.

"Good night, all," she said quickly before her voice could grow unsteady and give her away. Kit must not know about the hurt inside her. Never, ever!

"You *must* be tired, Marth," Ellen said. "How about you, Christine?"

"I'm tired too," Kit murmured.

She did not tell Ellen to call her Kit.

But she didn't tell me either till I asked her, Martha remembered.

50

She opened her eyes again. She had stopped wanting to cry. She watched Kit dig in her suitcase and come up with a pair of slippers.

What next? Martha wore slippers in the winter, and even then mostly when Mother told her to.

"Well," said Ellen to both of them, "Sweet dreams, and a pleasant repose, with a bundle of clothes, tucked under your nose."

Kit looked after her in astonishment. Martha quickly let her eyes almost close and pretended she was already asleep. Through the slits of space she had left open, she watched Kit turn to her, open her mouth, shut it again and bend over to put on the slippers.

Martha felt guilty.

But she wouldn't talk to me hardly, she argued with herself. Why should I explain Mother's Great-Aunt Jen taught her to say that? Let her see what it's like not to be talked to.

She closed her eyes properly so she could not see Kit even through her lashes. She heard Kit rummage in her suitcase again and then go out to the bathroom.

So she's brushing her teeth and washing her face . . . so what? Martha jeered silently. My teeth need a rest and I feel extremely clean.

Then she thought of her promise to Ellen to try to think of "some way out." By now she was sure

51

Chadron State College Library
Chadron, Nebraska

that she, Ellen and the Swanns could not enjoy living together at the cottage no matter how hard they tried. They were too different. It was that simple. But how could she get Mother to understand that? She would have to call home when nobody could overhear her end of the conversation. That was certain.

Kit came back, got into bed and turned off the light. Martha waited for her to say good night. Kit did not say a word.

Of course she thinks I'm really asleep, Martha remembered. She took long steady breaths. Then she heard Kit's breath catch. Was it only a sigh or was she crying?

Oh, if only I could have gone to camp, Martha thought, adding her aloneness to Kit's. If only Rosemary and Kit were different and we could have fun!

Then she buried her face in the pillow in case she turned out to be the one in tears and Kit the one who listened.

Martha woke up first. This was her chance. Mother was always up early. She would be sure to answer the phone and, with nobody around, Martha was almost sure she could explain things so that Mother would see how badly everything had gone wrong.

She slipped out of bed and went downstairs like a

shadow. Still trying to figure out just the right words to say, she hunched over the phone, dialing as quietly as she could. It rang only once.

"Hello. Toby Winston speaking."

Why, Martha moaned inwardly. Why Toby?

"Toby, let me speak to Mother."

"Is that you, Martha?"

"Yes, of course it is. Don't get smart. Call Mother."

"Well, she's sleeping, you know, Martha," Toby said doubtfully. "I just got up to go to the bathroom, but it's EARLY. The hand isn't at seven."

Martha glanced across the room at the clock and gasped.

A quarter to six!

"Toby . . . I'll call back later, I guess. Don't wake anybody up."

"I wasn't going to. It was YOUR idea," Toby pointed out.

"Okay, okay. And don't tell them I called," Martha said, having a sudden vision of him blurting it out in front of everybody at breakfast and Mother immediately calling the cottage and she, Martha, caught with the other three girls listening.

"Okay," Toby said, muffling a sudden yawn.

"What did I just tell you?"

"Don't wake Mother up and don't say anything about you . . . Hey, is this a secret, Martha? Is it

53

something about your camp?" Toby sounded wide-awake all at once.

"No!" Martha groaned. "Forget about me and go back to bed. It's EARLY. 'Bye."

Martha hung up on Toby's explaining that he had known all along it was early. She hoped he wouldn't tell. She thought she was probably safe, but you never knew what Toby took in and what he didn't. She had a glass of milk and then sneaked back up to bed. Lying there, watching the sunshine begin to inch its way into the room, she felt unaccountably happier. It was a new day. Maybe everything would have changed. She'd give them one more chance the way Mother always said. She grinned. It wasn't only Mother. She herself liked liking people better than disliking them. And these Swanns were mysterious in a way. Interesting. Maybe.

At nine o'clock, Ellen, Kit and Martha had finished breakfast. Rosemary had not yet appeared.

"She likes sleeping late," Kit volunteered, looking uncomfortable about it.

"Shall I leave everything out for her? What will she want?" Ellen asked.

Kit looked unhappier than ever.

"I don't know," she mumbled. "I mean, I eat with Dad and mostly Rosemary eats later with Mother. While we were driving up here, though, she said she was on a grapefruit diet."

"We don't have grapefruit. Would she settle for an orange?" Ellen's voice sounded crisp.

"I guess so. And black coffee—only she likes sugar in it. And dry toast—only she has to have peanut butter on it."

"I like peanut butter too," Martha said. "In fact, I LOVE it."

"Rosemary eats it for protein, she says," Kit explained.

There was a strained silence.

"Well, we'll do the best we can when she wakes up. We have lots of peanut butter," Ellen said. "Let's clear away our stuff."

The three of them made one too many in the small kitchen.

"You go and read or something, Christine. There isn't really room for all of us," Ellen said.

"I'd like to help," Kit offered.

"I'll read then," Martha said quickly.

Ellen gave her a dirty look and a clean dish towel.

"Forget it, Martha," she said, and to Kit, "You watch out, Christine, or Martha will run you ragged. She's an expert at landing somebody else with the work."

Kit, looking embarrassed, drifted away. Martha scowled.

"Gee whiz, Ellen, she SAID she wanted to help. It's important to make people feel needed."

"Yeah. That's why I'm letting you help instead.

I need you!" Ellen passed her the first of the juice glasses. Then she lowered her voice and made splashing noises to cover her next words.

"Have you thought of anything?"

Martha explained about the telephone call she had made and how she planned to try again the first chance she got.

"It'll be tricky," Ellen said, fishing out another juice glass.

Martha had not managed to dry the first one yet. She switched it till she held it in her left hand and used her good hand and arm for the polishing. She could do it but not well. She interrupted Ellen's train of thought.

"You know, it isn't easy drying dishes with a broken arm. Look how long it took me to do that one glass and it sure doesn't sparkle and shine the way Mother says they should."

"You're doing just fine," Ellen said, not even looking at the glass on the counter. Handing Martha the second one, she went on, "It'll be hard to get them out of the way so they'll be certain not to hear. I could take them out to the beach maybe—but suppose Rosemary forgot something! She might come in and catch you . . ."

"Good morning," Rosemary Swann said from right behind them.

"Oh, my!" Ellen said—and dropped a bread-and-butter plate.

5 | Only Till Wednesday

It didn't break. Rosemary stooped to pick it up. "Sorry I overslept," she said, giving it back to Ellen.

She didn't hear us, Martha thought with relief.

"That's okay. But we haven't any grapefruit." Ellen's words made sense but she sounded flustered. She hurried on, clearly hoping Rosemary was not noticing anything unusual. "We DO have peanut butter. And coffee—but only instant. Come on and I'll show you."

She dried her hands and led the way back to the breakfast table. Martha finished drying the second juice glass, dropped her dish towel and followed. She was not about to miss anything.

"I've decided that grapefruit diet isn't helping anyhow," Rosemary said, looking down at herself with an expression meant to be despairing. Martha looked too. As far as she could see, Rosemary did not carry a single extra ounce anywhere.

Who cares? Martha silently asked the world. Call

me Pudge. Call me Fatso. I ENJOY peanut butter!

She smiled then at her own thoughts and felt sorry for Rosemary worrying over nothing at all.

"You're supposed to be drying dishes, Martha," Ellen said.

"You're supposed to be washing," Martha countered, and sat down to watch Rosemary eat.

It was a disappointment. Rosemary had exactly what the rest of them had had.

"Drat!" Ellen said, looking past Martha through the front windows. "It's clouding over."

"It couldn't be going to rain!" Martha said in dismay, twisting around to see for herself.

Rainy days at the cottage were sometimes the nicest of all. But for their first day with the Swanns, she and Ellen needed sunshine and plenty of it. The clouds rolling up were not small, white and fluffy; they were a thick dismal grey and almost certainly filled with rain. Martha sighed.

"Where's Christine?" Rosemary asked, helping herself to another slice of toast, lathering it with butter, peanut butter and, finally, honey.

Some diet!

"I'll go find her," Martha said.

Kit was curled up on the chesterfield. She was so engrossed in the book she was reading that she did not look up till Martha plunked herself down beside her.

"Oh!" she said. Then, all in a rush, "I'm sorry.

I didn't ask if I could b-borrow this. But it's one of my favorite books. . . ."

Martha checked the cover. *A Little Princess* by Frances Hodgson Burnett.

"That's okay," she said. "I love it too. I've read it about two million times. Anyway, feel free to borrow any book you like."

They both smiled. Martha snuggled down into the couch cushions.

"This chesterfield is a perfect place for reading on a rainy day if Toby and Bruce aren't around to bother you," she said.

"Chesterfield?" Kit sounded puzzled.

Martha, just as puzzled, looked at her. "What do you mean, 'chesterfield?' " she asked.

"I mean what do *you* mean? The only chesterfields I've ever heard of are cigarettes," Kit said. Her voice shook on the last words.

Martha gave a big bounce that made the old springs creak. "This is a chesterfield. It's one of the best things in the cottage. You can bounce on it and put your feet up and nobody ever tells you to sit like a lady."

"Oh," Kit said. "I guess we say a sofa in America."

An awkward silence fell. Kit looked down at her book but did not begin reading again. Martha considered getting a book for herself but she did not feel like reading.

Then rain sounded on the roof above them.

"I'm going to build a fire in the fireplace," Martha said.

Rosemary helped Ellen with the rest of the dishes. When they came into the living room, Martha was struggling to arrange the logs properly. She was able to put the kindling in easily with one hand but the logs were too fat.

"Here. Let me," Ellen said.

"Where do you keep your records?" Rosemary asked. "You must have something decent."

Martha started up angrily but Ellen silenced her with a hand on her arm. "They're in that big box beside the chesterfield," she told Rosemary.

Not that again! Martha thought as Rosemary hesitated.

"It means sofa," Kit said, not looking up from her book.

"They've never heard of chesterfields," Martha told Ellen in a low voice as Rosemary located the record box.

The tone in which she read off the names of the first few albums she found made Martha mad all over again.

"*Mary Poppins . . . Black Beauty . . . Peter and the Wolf . . . The Nutcracker Suite . . . Love Songs for Friends and Foes . . .*"

"I think you might like that one," Ellen said. "It's an old Pete Seeger one of Mother's. I like it."

Rosemary flipped through the rest, gave a little

snort, pulled out the Pete Seeger album and went straight to the record player.

She must have spotted that last night, Martha thought.

"My friend Nancy Elliot has her own stereo in her bedroom up at their summer place in Maine," Rosemary said, placing the record on the turntable. "And you should see her record collection. She has EVERYTHING!"

"She must be an only child," Ellen said.

Rosemary raised her head in surprise.

"How did you know?" she asked.

Ellen grinned.

"Once I asked Mother why we didn't have more money for things like that, things we don't really need but still want, and she said she had given me a sister and two brothers instead. She asked me which one I wanted her to trade in."

"What did you say?" Martha demanded.

"Wouldn't you like to know!" Ellen said. She added, for Rosemary's benefit, "We do have a stereo in town. One for the whole family so it's in the living room. It's a pretty good one, though."

"That's what we have too," Kit put in unexpectedly. "We got it just last Christmas."

Rosemary said nothing more but started the record playing. Ellen struck a match and lit the fire. Rosemary came over and stretched out on the floor in front of it, listening to the music and gazing into the fire. Martha, watching her, realized that even though she did look like Mrs. Swann, Rosemary was really pretty, maybe even beautiful. The look of scorn, the hardness which had made Martha so sure she could never like this older girl, were gone now. Perhaps it was some magic worked by the firelight but Rosemary's face seemed filled with dreaming.

Open the door softly.
I've something to tell you, dear,

the voice on the record invited.

She's listening to whatever it is he has to say, thought Martha.

Then Ellen got up and fetched the new jigsaw puzzle Mother had bought the week before. She dumped it out on the card table by the window. It was a round puzzle and it looked almost impossible to do, but puzzles were good to work at on a rainy day, even if they weren't wildly exciting. Martha helped turn the pieces right side up and groaned as she saw dozens which looked exactly alike.

"It's over half blue sky," she complained. "And how do you know which are the edge pieces?"

"Courage, Marth. We don't have to go back to school till September," Ellen said.

"Don't laugh. It may take that long," Martha said, turning over three more blue pieces which appeared identical.

They were all quiet then for a while, the snapping of the fire and the soft but steady thrumming of the rain on the roof becoming a background for the songs Pete Seeger sang.

My young love came to me.
She moved through the fair.
So softly she wandered
both here and there. . . .

"I found two edge pieces that fit!" Martha cried in delight.

"Good," Ellen said. Then she straightened up for a second, stretched, looked around the room and laughed.

"What's so funny?" Martha asked. Rosemary looked up and even Kit raised her head although she was nearly in the middle of the book by now.

"It's nothing," Ellen said first. Then, as she saw they were all still waiting, she explained, "I just thought we look sort of like the girls in *Little Women*. When Marmee isn't there and they're grouped about in the parlor or whatever it was. Kit's smallest and quiet; she might be Beth. And you look like Meg, Rosemary. Except she wouldn't be wearing slacks."

"I absolutely refuse to be Amy, so forget it!" Martha said.

"It was so preachy that I never finished it," Rosemary said, tossing her hair back. "But Meg was okay. Elegant, wasn't she?"

"Stuck up," corrected Martha. "I skipped the preachy parts and I liked the rest. Those girls sounded as though they had a good time, putting on plays together. I liked Beth getting the piano and Jo jumping fences. I liked *Little Men* better though. Lots more happened."

"Still, the March girls did sound cozy, exactly the way we look right this minute." Ellen picked up her first train of thought. "Now all we need is to have Marmee come bustling in with a letter from Father at the Front."

"Or Laurie dropping by," Rosemary said. "I do remember Laurie."

"But Meg wasn't interested in Laurie," Ellen started to correct her. "She liked . . ."

A car horn sounded three short beeps outside. Martha stared at Ellen.

"That's Mother's honk," she said, her eyes wide.

All four of them were so startled that nobody moved before their two mothers came dashing in out of the rain and discovered them.

"How lovely!" Mrs. Swann cried, undoing her rain hat. "The nasty weather isn't bothering you clever girls one little bit."

Rosemary turned off the record player. Kit put down her book. Martha and Ellen exchanged glances.

64

Tell Mother somehow, Ellen commanded without speaking.

How? What? When? Where? Martha signaled back frantically.

But any tension was hidden in the flickering firelight. And the next moment, it was too late. The women had come not to see if their daughters were all right but to tell them that they themselves had spent the night before phoning old college friends and now they were setting out on a three-day trip to visit a couple of them.

"But we did want to be certain first that you were getting along fine. Mrs. Hammond is baby-sitting the boys when your father is away and they aren't involved in the Park Summer Recreation Program. So call her if you need help," Caroline Winston said. She was beginning to look hard at Martha. Martha was unusually quiet.

Ellen kicked Martha's ankle.

"Hey, that sounds great!" Martha said, trying to sound as though she meant it but feeling certain her mother would not be fooled. "When do you leave?"

"We've already left," her mother said, smiling at her. "The cottage was right along our route, so we have our suitcases in the car and I'm sorry but we can't stay or we won't get there in time for supper."

"My goodness!" was the best Martha could manage.

Mrs. Swann beamed around at all four of them.

"I've been telling Caroline that I know my two girls, and I think you'll be wanting to return to civilization when we come back on Wednesday," she said. "I thought you'd be longing to come home already, Rosemary, to the bright lights and the boys. But I must say you look as snug as a bug in a rug."

"Well, we ARE having fun, of course," Rosemary said, not looking at the Winston girls, "but maybe, by Wednesday, we'd like a change. Who knows?"

"Yeah. Who knows?" Martha echoed.

"What about you, Ellen?" Mother asked. "How's everything going?"

"Fine. Just fine," Ellen assured her. "But Mrs. Swann could be right about three days being long enough. I mean, if it goes on raining all the time . . . you know!"

"We'll hope for fine weather for you," Mother said, her voice slowing a little as she studied her daughters' faces. "We'll be sure to come on Wednesday. However, as Nell says, you do look very cozy."

Martha kept her smile fixed in place although she wanted to yell at her mother that Wednesday was a hundred years away and please, please, rescue them now, this minute!

She waited for somebody to ask Kit's opinion. Not that it would help. Nobody did.

Mrs. Swann put her rain hat back on. There was a chorus of good-byes. The women left, talking happily as they went.

66

When the girls heard the car pull away, nobody knew what to say. In the last few minutes, they had all realized that none of them wanted to be there shut up together in a cottage by themselves. But here they were and here they clearly had to stay. Ellen switched on a stand lamp, for it was getting too dark to work at the puzzle. Rosemary lifted the arm of the record player and carefully placed the needle at the place where she had taken it off.

Little girl, little girl, see through my window.
Little girl, little girl, see through my window.

Pete Seeger sang.

Then Kit amazed them all by breaking into a low laugh.

"*Little Women*," she explained, still laughing, when the other three looked at her. "That is exactly the way they saw us. Grouped around the fireside."

"As dear Bethie said, 'Birds in their little nests agree. Why can't we?' " Martha quoted, mocking the words. Then she, too, laughed. "I still refuse to be that snippety Amy," she declared.

"We can't all be Jo," Ellen said. "She's the only one with a good part. She was practically liberated in spite of her long skirts."

Rosemary sat up, hugging her knees. She was not laughing at all.

"But we aren't," she said. "Liberated, that is.

We're cooped up in here and all we can do is what the song says—see through the window."

They looked. The grey rain fell steadily, darkening and blurring the world. The bright moment Kit's laughter had created ended.

Then Rosemary went to search for another record. Kit escaped back to Sara Crewe's attic where magical things were about to happen. Martha hunted halfheartedly for another puzzle piece.

"I didn't make my bed yet," Ellen said, standing up. "Did you, Martha?"

"I can't very well with this arm," Martha said. "Anyway I like getting into my bed just the way I left it, and Mother isn't here."

"Okay. Be a slob," Ellen said, starting for the stairs.

"It's only till Wednesday," Rosemary reminded her.

"It won't be all that bad," Ellen said.

She was no longer talking about bedmaking.

"If only it stops raining!" Martha said.

"Yeah," Rosemary said. "I have to work on my tan."

But the rain did not stop until suppertime. It was a long day.

6 | Night Visitor

After supper they went for a walk down the beach. After the dark, wet day, the sunset seemed incredibly lovely. The girls did not say much as they set out, but they all drew in big breaths of the clean, cool air. Martha, feeling set free, kept breaking into skips and jumps of joy. Finally she settled for walking backward.

"I can see the sunset much better this way," she told the others.

Kit watched her for a minute or two and then turned and fell in beside her.

"Nancy Elliot's place is beautiful but it doesn't have a beach like this," Rosemary said to Ellen. "They take lawn chairs out on their patio though and it's built up on a cliff so you get a tremendous view."

She paused.

"It must be lovely," Ellen said.

Rosemary looked back over her shoulder and caught her breath at the glory of the fiery streaks of gold above the horizon and their tumbled brightness reflected in the water. When she faced forward again, Martha saw her expression change from one of wonder to a scowl.

"Of course, we see the ocean there instead of just a lake," Rosemary said. Her voice sharpened. "Christine, turn around and walk properly. You'll fall, not looking where you're going."

Kit hesitated.

"What's eating you? The sand won't hurt her if she does fall," Martha answered back.

"Martha, don't be rude," Ellen said.

Kit took a couple more steps and then did as Rosemary had told her.

Rosemary ignored Martha's remark. Kit trailed along, no longer bothering to look back at the beauty of the sky. Martha continued to walk backward, taking care not to lose her footing. She couldn't tell the Swann girls what she thought of them, not without really being rude, but she could speak her mind to Ellen.

"Just because you're older doesn't make you my boss," she said.

"I'm not bossing you," Ellen answered quietly. "I think it's time we started back. The sun's gone down and it'll get dark fast now."

"Are there any shows around here?" Rosemary asked when they were nearly home.

"None we can walk to," Ellen said.

Rosemary gave a loud sigh. "Nancy has her own car," she said.

"There's a bowling alley," Martha told her.

"Martha, it's practically five miles away," Ellen exclaimed.

"I know," Martha said, "but if she's so desperate . . . !"

"We don't go there any more even when the car's here," Ellen told Rosemary. "It used to be fun but now a whole gang of tough kids hangs around there. The police have been out a couple of times already this summer breaking up fights and stuff. Dad won't take us there any longer."

"Are any of the boys good-looking?" Rosemary drawled.

There was a short silence while Ellen opened the door of the cottage and turned on a light. Then she turned to face Rosemary.

"I wasn't interested enough to notice," Ellen said. "Maybe you can get your mother to drive you over on Thursday night so you can look for yourself."

Wow! Martha thought. And she called ME rude!

Rosemary laughed. "I was only kidding," she said. "Who cares about the boys around here? We're leaving on Wednesday."

"Of course," Ellen said. "What would you like to do now?"

"I started a book this afternoon," Rosemary said. "I'd like to finish it, if nobody minds, that is."

Everyone had a book she wanted to go on with. Martha was rereading *The Secret Language*. It was one of her favorite books because the most interesting character in it was also named Martha. Kit was now into Rosemary Sutcliff's *Warrior Scarlet*. Ellen was halfway through a library book called *Bright Island*.

"What are you reading?" Ellen asked Rosemary.

"It's a paperback I found on the table by my bed. *Julie of the Wolves*," Rosemary said.

"That's a great book," Ellen said. "I loaned it to Mother and she liked it too. When you're finished, I have lots of others you can borrow."

They smiled at each other.

Now they're almost friends, Martha decided in surprise. And Kit's not bad either. Three days will be gone before we know it.

But you wanted to make it a camp, a voice inside reminded her.

Martha didn't listen.

This time she brushed her teeth when Kit did and, when they decided to quit reading and turn out the light, they both said, "Good night."

Sometime in the night, Martha woke up with a start. It was very dark. She had no idea what had wakened her but something had.

"Kit?" she said.

Kit made no answer. Martha's eyes were getting used to the darkness. Now she could see the window at the foot of Kit's bed. She rolled over onto her back. Then she heard it—a sound that did not belong—and half remembered it breaking into her sleep. She pushed herself up on her elbows and looked around. There was a small, bunched-up thing on the window screen right beside her bed. Martha stiffened. What . . . what was it?

It moved.

For one second, she thought it was trying to get in at her. The next, it doubled in size as it launched itself right over her and across the room in a giant swoop.

A bird! You dope, it's just a little bird, Martha thought wildly.

The thing swung through the darkness again, returning to the screen. It did not fly like a bird.

Martha tried not to remember *The Flying Fingers of Doom*. She had seen it one night when her parents were out and Ellen let her stay up and watch *The Late Show*. Somebody's hand had been chopped off and it thirsted for revenge and somehow it grew wings and came in the night and opened people's windows and murdered them while they slept.

"Kit," Martha called hoarsely. "Kit, wake up!"

"Why?" Kit said from the depths of sleep.

"There's a flying thing in here," Martha quavered.

"Martha," Kit said slowly, "is that you?"

"Oh, wake up!" Martha cried.

"I am awake." Kit raised her head and peered through the darkness trying to find Martha. The Flying Fingers of Doom spread itself out in the air, circled the room and landed back on Martha's screen.

Kit screamed and dove under her blankets.

"EL-LEN!" Martha yelled. Then she, too, hauled her covers over her head.

Nothing happened. Had that thing dropped down on top of her? Was it crawling up to find her head?

Martha strained her ears for sounds of Ellen coming. She could hear only the thudding of her own heart. She slid her good arm out, groped around on the floor and found her sneaker.

Armed, she poked her head out. There was no shadow on either screen. Shoe in hand, Martha sat up slowly. There was no movement anywhere.

"Now listen here," Martha said.

The thing dove straight at her. Paralyzed, Martha let the sneaker fall from her nerveless hand. The monster missed her by inches and was back clinging to the wire mesh.

"ELLEN!!!" This time there was sheer terror in her shriek.

The first call had fitted itself into a dream Ellen was having. The second brought her out of bed in one bound. Charging into the hall, she ran into Rosemary.

"What is it? What's the matter?" Rosemary demanded.

"I don't know yet." Ellen rushed past her to Martha's door.

"What on earth . . . ?" she said into the shadows.

"Oh, Ellen," Martha moaned. "It's not a bird. Remember that monster hand on TV? . . . Oooooh, there it goes!"

Ellen leaped backward, landing on Rosemary's toes.

"You idiot, Martha!" she said when she got her breath. "It's just a bat, that's all."

"A . . . a bat?"

"Put on your light. See if I ever let you watch another horror movie!"

Martha switched on the light above her bed. She had always loved animals. Rats, mice, snakes, lizards, turtles, toads. . . . Why not bats? In all the years they had been coming to the cottage, this was the first time a bat had blundered in. She spotted him on the rafters. He looked dried-up and wrinkled, a dark crumpled shape, too small to hurt anybody.

Kit was still hiding under her blankets.

"Come on out!" Martha said in scorn, as though she herself had never for one instant thought of *The Flying Fingers of Doom*. "It's nothing to get into such a snit over. Bats are perfectly harmless, aren't they, Ellen?"

"It might bite if it was cornered." Ellen stayed close to the door.

"You kill them with a broom," Rosemary volunteered.

"The broom's downstairs." Ellen eyed the dark stairwell.

"I'll come with you," Rosemary said.

"Hey, wait! You can't do that!" Martha's voice, loud with outrage, made them pause. "He's probably already terrified because he can't get out. That's why he keeps going to the window."

"You explain to him that the screens are hooked on from the outside," Ellen said. "We'll be right back."

She and Rosemary departed. Martha turned back to the hump in the other bed where Kit was still playing possum.

"Kit, come out RIGHT NOW!" she ordered. "They're going to kill him!"

Kit stuck her head halfway out. Martha by this time was standing on her bed, staring up at the corner where the bat had taken refuge. Trying to see better, she jumped up into the air. When she landed with a jarring bounce, the bat dropped from the rafter. He came so close to Martha before he veered that she saw his tiny ratlike face. Forgetting her broken arm, she collapsed onto her bed.

"I saw him up close," she panted. "He's like a squirrel only . . . only . . ." Her voice shuddered to a stop.

She joined Kit in a new retreat under the bedclothes.

Rosemary and Ellen arrived with the broom.

"Here," Rosemary said, grabbing a towel from the hall bannister. "You put this around your head to keep them out of your hair."

"They don't go in your hair," Martha said from beneath her sheet. "I read in a magazine that that's an old wives' tale."

Ellen paid no attention to her. She held out the broom and towel to Rosemary.

"You know how. You do it," she said.

"It's your house," Rosemary began. Then she relented. "Okay. I'll try."

Blinded by the towel, she came in swinging. The bat flapped, glided, squeaked but stayed out of reach.

"Ouch!" Martha yelped as the broom cracked down on her leg.

"Your turn," Rosemary said to Ellen and handed over towel and broom.

Ellen also missed the bat by miles. She got Kit once and Martha twice more.

Then, freeing herself from the towel, she looked for the bat. Rosemary peered over her shoulder.

No bat on either window. No leathery huddle of wings up near the roof.

"I'm positive he didn't fly out past me," Rosemary stated, her voice going shrill at the very thought.

"He moves pretty fast," Ellen said. "Martha! Christine! He's gone."

Martha emerged slowly, her face screwed up.

"You mean, you . . . you . . . murdered . . ."

"No, dimbulb. He got away," Ellen said.

"Are you sure?" Kit asked, coming out for air.

They looked. The bat was nowhere to be found.

"I'm going to bed," said Rosemary. "Christine, you get up and come in with me."

For once, Kit spoke up.

"Not me," she said. "He's probably hiding in YOUR room."

Martha grinned at the shock on the older girls' faces.

"Please shut the door when you leave," she said.

"You little wretches." Ellen linked arms with Rosemary. "Come on. I'll help you search."

Martha and Kit heard furniture being bumped about, and the sound of the other girls' voices.

"He must have gone downstairs," Ellen said at last. "Close your door."

"I'm putting a chair against it," Rosemary said.

Martha turned the light out but both she and Kit were too excited to sleep right away.

"You were awfully brave, Marth," Kit said, breaking the friendly silence.

Martha thought of how petrified she had really been. If Kit had been watching instead of hiding, she would know. But it was over now. Martha did not have to tell.

"You know what you said about getting out of going to camp?" she said instead.

"Yeah," Kit said, mystified but ready to listen.

"I was supposed to go to camp yesterday," Martha told her. "If I hadn't broken my arm . . ."

She spilled out the whole story. Only one thing

she held back. She told Kit that she was the one who first suggested they stay at the cottage but she did not mention telling Bruce that they would have a camp of their own there. Kit would only think she was crazy the way Ellen did.

"I'm sorry," Kit murmured when Martha had finished. "I mean, I'm sorry about you breaking your arm and not getting to go to camp. I'm glad you're here though."

Martha was not sure what to answer. She liked Kit better now but she still was not glad she had had to stay at the cottage.

"Well, I guess . . ." she began.

Thump! Thump!

The hollow banging on the far side of the room drove all thought of camp out of her mind.

"He's back!" Kit cried. "It's that bat! Oh, I wish I HAD gone to camp. I'd give anything to be there. This place is AWFUL!!!"

"Be quiet," Martha ordered and switched the light on again. She waited. Another thump sounded. She slipped out of bed and crept toward the source of the noise.

"I see him. He's in the wastepaper basket," she told Kit in a voice that shook only a little. "He must have fallen in and knocked himself out. Now he's come to and doesn't know how to escape. I don't think he can fly straight up."

Kit did not answer. Martha herself was not sure of

what bats could or could not do. She backed up and thought. The next instant, Kit heard a different bang.

"I've got him!" Martha said, right out loud.

Kit did not move a muscle.

"Come on out and see. He's trapped. He can't hurt you."

Cautiously, Kit emerged.

There sat Martha on the wastebasket, grinning, her sling at a rakish angle.

"Wh-where is he?"

"Under me," Martha laughed. "But there's a book in between. One of the boys' picture books. Hurry up. I need your help."

"But what are we going to do?" Kit squeaked.

"We're going to take him downstairs and let him go outside," Martha announced, as though setting bats free was all in a night's work to her. "You hold the basket up underneath. That takes two hands. And I'll hold this book steady."

She stood up, glanced down at the book and burst out laughing. Kit sat and stared at her.

"Look at which book I grabbed." Martha chuckled. "I didn't pick it on purpose, but it's perfect."

Kit came to see. It was a copy of *Where the Wild Things Are*. She smiled in spite of herself.

They went in the dark to keep Ellen and Rosemary out of it.

Halfway down the stairs, the basket slipped in Kit's clammy hands. For one second, there was a bigger-than-bat-sized gap between basket and book. Kit almost dropped everything and ran, but Martha's sharp whisper sliced through her panic.

"Hold on and KEEP IT UP!"

Kit managed to obey. A couple of times they bumped against the wall as they went, but no light came on above them. They were at the bottom of the stairs. They were crossing the living room.

"Hold-on-and-keep-it-up. Hold-on-and-keep-it-up," Kit whispered, using the words as a charm.

They reached the French doors. Martha made sure the book was balanced and let go. With difficulty she got the bolt to move, the key to turn.

It was done. Hardly breathing, they went out into the night. The wind caught at their pajamas. The sand under their bare feet felt damp and cold.

"Now put it down . . . carefully!"

Kit went down on her knees, easing the basket onto the ground. Martha stepped back, taking the book with her. Kit leaped to stand beside her.

They waited, watching the basket. A full minute went by. Nothing happened. Not even a thump.

"Maybe he's dead," Kit whispered.

"Idiot," Martha said. "Stand back a bit."

Kit promptly backed up six feet. Martha picked up a stick, a hobby horse of Toby's left lying by the door. She reached out with it. Over the basket went!

They almost missed seeing the bat, he glided so swiftly, so soundlessly into freedom. He wheeled, a small shadow against the stars. He was gone.

Martha blinked, but the sky waited there, empty. She turned to Kit, now at her side.

"Wasn't that . . . great?" she whispered.

Kit nodded.

There were no words big enough to say how wonderful it had been.

The rescuers stood together, staring up into the mystery of the night, feeling the openness, the cool air moving on their cheeks.

Then something rustled in the bushes a few feet away from them. They whirled around. Martha grabbed the wastebasket. Kit snatched up the book. They raced for the cottage.

Safe inside, Martha paused to relock the door. Then the two of them sped up the stairs and into bed. Kit did not say anything. Martha too lay silent, feeling joy spread through her like a wave of light.

Soon she heard Kit breathing evenly, as though she had fallen asleep right away.

"Farewell, bat!" Martha said. "Go home to your wife and children. Stay out of houses. Especially ours."

"Whoever heard of a bat with a wife and children?" Kit laughed, startling Martha so she jumped. "Do you think he'll tell them about us rescuing him in a wastepaper basket?"

Martha felt foolish, but she relaxed, hearing understanding in Kit's words.

"You never know," she answered. "Who can tell how bats think and talk to each other?"

There was a companionable silence. Then Kit spoke again.

"Martha . . ."

"Yeah?" Martha said when Kit stalled.

"I didn't really mean that about wishing I'd gone to camp," Kit said.

"That's good," Martha said.

There was a pause. Then Kit asked, "How about you?"

"I'm really glad I was here tonight," Martha said. She could not say more than that. She still wished with all her heart that she had been able to go to camp.

But the night's adventure had changed everything for Martha. She could have fun with Kit and Ellen until Wednesday, even though Rosemary was a pain in the neck.

"It won't be so bad," Martha promised. "We can swim and stuff. A bit dull maybe. I mean, we won't save a bat every night."

Kit squealed at the very thought and Martha laughed at her. Five minutes later, they were both asleep.

7 | I'm a Canadian!

Martha opened her eyes, took one delighted look at the blue sky outside her small window and swung her feet out of bed. Turning to reach for her bathing suit, she saw Kit watching her.

"Hi," Martha said, shedding her pajamas.

"G-good morning," Kit returned, snuggling into her covers.

"Aren't you coming?" Martha demanded in amazement.

"Coming where?"

"Out on the beach. Swimming if the water's not too cold. It's a beautiful morning," Martha said.

Kit slowly pushed back her bedclothes and sat up.

"Hurry," Martha urged.

Kit put on a burst of speed for an instant, but then slowed down again. She studied Martha.

"Does your whole family get up like that?" she asked.

"Like what?"

"Shooting right out of bed the minute their eyes open. I was awake first. I saw you."

Martha laughed.

"Toby's even faster than I am," she said. "The rest poke. Ellen is hopeless."

Kit seemed glad to hear she was not the only one in Martha's world who failed to meet the day as though it were a bugle sounding "Charge!" Yet Martha's eagerness was catching.

Kit hurried. Still, it seemed to Martha to take her forever before she was ready. When she had her trim blue bathing suit on, she reached for a comb.

"Why bother?" Martha asked. "We'll be swimming."

"I always comb my hair in the morning," Kit said, and went ahead.

Then she left to wash her face. Martha, who had rubbed the sleep out of her eyes and felt that was sufficient, made no comment this time. Arguing would only make Kit take longer.

Kit returned and took thongs, a blue bathing cap and a matching blue towel from her suitcase.

"Okay," she said. "I'm ready."

Martha, who had never worn a bathing cap in her life, who didn't match unless she was dressed up for church or a party, and who went barefoot on the sand, led the way.

I wonder if she's this good every minute, she thought uneasily as they reached the bottom of the stairs.

Then they were at the glass doors and Martha was looking out at the lake, sand and sky.

"It is a perfect day," she declared. "Absolutely perfect. Wait here a second." With no further explanation, she left.

"Here," she said, reappearing.

Kit looked down in astonishment at what she was being offered. Two chocolate marshmallow cookies and a celery stick! Kit Swann had never, since babyhood, started a day without orange juice, a bowl of cereal, a piece of toast and a glass of milk. Sometimes she had eggs and bacon. Once in a long while, there were pancakes. But never, never cookies and celery!

"This isn't breakfast," Martha answered her startled look. "It's just to keep us going till Ellen gets up."

Martha began devouring her own selection. A raw carrot, a chocolate cookie like Kit's and a date square! She glanced up and caught Kit watching wide-eyed.

"Go on. Try it," Martha invited.

Kit cautiously bit into a cookie.

"Well?"

"It's good," Kit admitted, and then crunched on the celery.

Martha finished the date square in one enormous mouthful and started toward the water.

"Are you going to wear your sling in?" Kit asked.

Martha nodded. "The doctor said I should. After a day or two, he said. Well, one day's up. I have an extra sling."

"But won't it hurt to swim?" Kit asked.

"I'll do it with just one arm," Martha said. "I'll be okay. Come on."

Kit paused to put on her bathing cap. Martha watched her tucking her carefully combed hair up under it. Then curiosity got the better of her.

"Why do you wear that?" she asked.

"Pardon?" Kit said, unable to hear through the rubber cap.

"WHY WEAR A BATHING CAP?"

Kit looked at Martha for a minute and then suddenly, to Martha's surprise, she pulled the cap back off and dropped it by the towels.

"I only wondered why," Martha said. "I mean, you have straight, shortish hair and I thought . . ."

"You have to wear them at the pool at home," Kit said. "But I can't hear with it on. And Mother's not here to say anything."

Martha smiled at her. "Let's go," she said.

The two of them ran toward the water. They slowed down at the edge and tried it. It was freezing.

"You just have to go in fast," Martha said bravely, and waded in up to her waist. Kit splashed in behind her.

"It's like Morning Dip," she said through chattering teeth.

"What?" Martha asked.

"Morning Dip—at camp," Kit explained. "They have it before breakfast. It's awful."

Then she took a deep breath and ducked under. Martha's face lighted.

"Great!" she cried and pushed off with both feet. Immediately her sling became wet and heavy. She rolled sideways, going off course. But it didn't hurt and she was in swimming. However, the water was icy. She headed for shore.

Kit beat her to the spot where their towels waited and bundled herself up. In spite of her clammy sling, Martha could see she was not as cold as Kit.

"Your lips are purple," she observed.

Kit hugged her towel closer. "They always get that way," she agreed.

Martha plunked herself down on the sand and sighed.

"When you're fifteen pounds overweight, your fat keeps you warm," she said, dropping her towel.

Kit looked sideways at her.

"You don't look fifteen pounds overweight," she murmured.

"I am, though," stated Martha. "I do like to eat. Though maybe I won't now Ellen's doing the cooking."

"Can't she cook?"

"She's okay with mixes and stuff," Martha said. "But she needs a cookbook for foods that don't come in packages."

"What's wrong with that?" Kit asked.

"Mother doesn't keep a cookbook at the cottage,

and when she brought you guys out, she forgot to bring one. I guess Ellen can really do most ordinary things we'd want. Anyway, Mother brought piles of food, so we won't starve."

"I wasn't worried," Kit said, "although Rosemary can't cook either. Mrs. Neville won't let her near the kitchen."

"Who's Mrs. Neville?"

"Our housekeeper," Kit said.

Martha's eyes widened.

"Your housekeeper!" she said. "Boy, I knew Americans were rich but I didn't know they had housekeepers. Is she like Mrs. Medlock in *The Secret Garden?*"

Kit stared at her.

"Mrs. Neville's a lady who lives up the street from us," she said slowly. "She comes in every afternoon to clean and get dinner because Mother doesn't get home from work till after six. She's fat and bossy and always in a hurry to get home. She is not one bit like Mrs. Medlock."

"Oh," Martha said, feeling both put in her place and disappointed. The Swanns' "housekeeper" sounded exactly like the woman who worked for Tracey's family. Tracey's mother was a lawyer.

"What kind of job does your mother have?" she asked.

"She runs a travel bureau," Kit said.

Martha nodded and lost interest.

"Let's build a sand castle," she said. "I always

have to do it with Bruce and Toby and they won't do it my way. If I do get a good part done, Toby bombs it."

Kit still kept her towel snuggled around her, but she managed to help. Martha had trouble, since she could only use one hand. Yet between them, they produced a masterpiece of a castle. When the whole thing was as complete as they could make it, she went into the cottage again and came running back with a tiny Canadian flag. She stuck it on top of the tallest tower of all. The wind flicked it so that it flew proudly. Martha stood, feet set apart, her right hand on her hip, and beamed at it. Then she looked at Kit.

"We don't have an American flag," she apologized.

"That's okay. This isn't America," Kit reminded her.

Martha sat back down.

"It's North America," she said, a touch of defiance in her voice.

Kit looked muddled. Martha tried to make her meaning clearer.

"It isn't the United States of America," she said. "But it sounds conceited calling yourselves Americans when we're Americans too, really."

Kit shoved her hair back with a gritty hand. "Do you want me to call you an American then?" she asked.

"Heck, no!" Martha said, stung. "I'm Canadian!"

The two of them stared at each other. They were both puzzled and a bit embarrassed by the whole conversation. Suddenly Kit leaned forward and patted smooth the top of the tunnel, which was already as smooth as hands could make it. Not looking at Martha, she blurted, "Wouldn't you like to be an American if you could?"

"Me!" Martha exclaimed. "An American! Not on your life! They think they're so wonderful, shoving their way . . ."

Her voice broke off abruptly. Kit stopped pretending to work on the castle. Her eyes, meeting Martha's, had a dangerous glint in them.

"I'm sorry," Martha mumbled, looking away. "You aren't like that. I don't know what made me say it. I never really knew an American before, not to talk to."

"Well, I never knew a Canadian before either," Kit said. She laughed suddenly. "Not to rescue bats with," she added.

Martha laughed too. Then there was silence, neither of them sure what to say next.

"And I only have one dollar and seventy-five cents!" Kit said.

"I knew you were rich," Martha shot back. "I've just got a dollar."

The cottage door banged, saving them.

"There's Ellen," Martha cried. "Come on. Breakfast!" And they raced in.

"We've already been in swimming," Martha bragged after Ellen had said grace. "It was great, wasn't it, Kit? The water was downright warm."

"I'll just bet," Ellen said, pouring milk on her cereal.

Kit was already eating hers. She glanced up in surprise at Martha's words, but said nothing. She bent her head over her bowl again, and spooned up another mouthful.

Puzzled by Kit's lack of response, Martha went on talking. "Kit said it was like Morning Dip at camp, Ellen," she said.

"When I was at camp, I never once went to Morning Dip," Rosemary said. "I remember one time they said that the next morning every single person had to come and I was horrified."

"But didn't you like it when you went?" Martha asked.

"I didn't go. I said I had a stomachache and I got to stay in bed in the infirmary all morning. It was neat," Rosemary said. "Everybody was so worried about me, and I loved having the chance to stay in bed."

"That was sneaky," Martha said slowly.

Rosemary smiled, remembering. "I'll say it was," she said, mistaking Martha's judgment for a compliment.

"If I went to camp, I wouldn't want to miss one minute of it," Martha declared.

It was not fair. Rosemary and Kit went to camp and she . . .

Martha suddenly began eating her own cereal ravenously.

"Christine," Rosemary said, "did you comb your hair after you came in from swimming?"

Martha glanced at Kit and then gave Rosemary a hard look. Of course Kit hadn't combed her hair. Anybody could see that. There was still some sand clinging to it where she had pushed it back.

"Yes," Kit said, not looking up.

"Are you sure?" Rosemary pressed on. "It certainly doesn't look like it. Mother says it is only polite to come to the table looking presentable, you know."

"More toast, Rosemary?" Ellen broke in.

"No. I'm dieting, really," Rosemary said. She turned back to her sister. "Are you listening to me, Christine?"

Kit nodded her head and then took a long drink of milk so she did not have to speak. Martha decided it was time to end the whole thing. Kit was dumb to have lied, but Martha could see now that she had been hoping to get out of the lecture Rosemary was beginning. Who did Rosemary think she was—God?

"Why should she comb it anyway, if she doesn't feel like it? It looks presentable to me. I definitely did NOT comb mine. The wind'll just tangle it again when we go back out," Martha said.

Rosemary glared at Martha, but Martha did not

flush and stare at her plate. She gave back glare for glare.

Rosemary looked away first. "Aren't children impossible?" she said to Ellen.

"I think they're okay," Ellen said.

Martha grinned. "What are we going to do today, Ellen?" she asked her sister.

Ellen jumped. She was not used to being the person in charge.

"We'll have to walk to the store," she planned aloud. "We're out of bread and milk, and we'll need other stuff."

"I have a broken arm," Martha said. "I can't carry parcels."

"There's nothing wrong with your other arm," Ellen told her.

Martha did not argue. She had no intention of staying home.

"Let's get pork chops," she suggested. "They're my favorite thing. They're easy, aren't they?"

Ellen stood up quickly and started clearing the table.

"I'll decide when we get there," she said briskly. "It depends on what he has."

As the four of them set off down the beach, the whole world glittered around them. The waves sparkled. The sky was its most vivid blue. Martha exulted in the brightness of it all, but Rosemary suddenly announced, "I really can't stand this glare. And I've left my sunglasses back in the cabin."

Cabin! Martha thought. The nerve of her!

"We'll turn back. We haven't come far," Ellen said.

"No, no. Christine can run back and fetch them. She hasn't done anything for anyone but herself this morning," Rosemary said.

"There was nothing to do." Ellen looked shocked at the harshness in Rosemary's voice.

"I'll get them," Kit mumbled. She started to run back the way they had come.

"Wait!" Ellen called, fishing in the pocket of her jeans. "She doesn't have the key."

"I'll take it. We'll catch up with you. Where are your dumb old glasses?" Martha was as rude as she knew how to be.

"Well, really!" exclaimed Rosemary.

"It'll take us a while to search the whole cottage, even if it is only a cabin to you," Martha snapped.

"They're in the pocket of my beach robe," Rosemary said in a subdued voice. Martha hoped she felt ashamed.

She should, she fumed, pounding along in Kit's wake.

They did not say anything when Martha caught up. They found the glasses easily.

"We'd better hurry," Kit said, as they locked the cottage again. "When Rosemary wants something, she wants it that minute."

"I wouldn't let her talk to me like that," Martha burst out. "You should have told her to get her own glasses. She was the one who forgot them."

"You don't know Rosemary," Kit said dully. "She's like Mother. And I didn't help with breakfast."

"There wasn't room in the kitchen," Martha said. "You can do the dishes later. I'll bet Rosemary hardly ever helps with dishes. Probably doesn't know how."

They trudged on. The others had stopped to wait. Just before they got close enough to be overheard, Kit murmured, "We have a dishwasher. She can work it perfectly."

Martha giggled.

Rosemary held out her hand. Kit handed over the glasses. They started to walk again. Martha could not stand it.

"You're very welcome, Rosemary," she said in a sugar-sweet voice.

"Oh," Rosemary said. "I guess I did forget to say thank you. Thanks, Christine."

"Martha found them," Kit said.

Rosemary had nothing to say to that. They kept going.

Then Martha noticed the wind was rising. She pranced in sudden excitement, scuffing up sand.

"Ellen, I think maybe we're in for a Big Blow," she announced.

"I wouldn't be surprised," Ellen said, studying the darkening water, the scudding clouds.

"What's a Big Blow?" Rosemary asked. She made the words sound silly, but Martha knew that Rosemary was the foolish one. You did not belittle a Big Blow.

"You'll see," Martha promised her. "The waves pile up till they're like crashing mountains. Everything goes wild. You can hardly stand up even, and you can't hear a thing but the roaring wind. Usually it lasts for three days. It's terrific."

Kit looked sick.

"What's wrong with you?" Martha asked her.

Kit didn't answer, but Rosemary rushed in with an explanation. She sounded exactly like Mrs. Swann.

"Poor Christine's terrified of storms," Rosemary said. "We're hoping she'll outgrow it. She even hides in her closet. She's really a bit of a baby about them."

"Anyway, Martha, you're exaggerating," Ellen protested quickly. "It's crazy to say you can hardly stand up."

Kit looked comforted. Martha opened her mouth to say that you certainly had to brace yourself at least, but she decided they would not believe her. They would find out, though. Rosemary was awful, talking about Kit like that. Still, Kit sounded more than a bit babyish. Hiding in her closet!

She was still thinking about it when they arrived at the store.

"What happened to your arm, Martha?" Mr. Doyle asked.

Martha showed off her sling and explained. Ellen began choosing fruit. Rosemary picked up a basket to help her. Kit stayed with Martha.

Martha looked around. In a glass case near her sat several thick pork chops.

"We want pork chops," she said. "Ellen is doing the cooking."

"Martha!" Ellen cried, too late. Mr. Doyle had taken the chops out of the case.

"How many do you need?" he asked Ellen.

Ellen hesitated.

"Four, please," Martha said.

She turned then and caught sight of her sister's face.

"Don't you know how to cook pork chops, Ellen?" Martha asked across the room. "We could have hot dogs or Kraft Dinner. I like them too and they're easy."

Mr. Doyle grinned at that. The other people in the store were listening with interest. Even Rosemary looked amused. Ellen raised her chin several notches. Ignoring her sister, she spoke directly to the man behind the counter.

"Four will be fine," she said.

8 | Martha Surprises Kit

"Hey," Martha said, forgetting pork chops. "He's made peanut brittle."

Mr. Doyle laughed at her as she hung over the display case, feasting her eyes on the candy.

"Knew you'd be in, Martha," he said.

"Ellen, look!" Martha cried.

"You, Martha Winston, need peanut brittle like a hole in the head," Ellen said, getting revenge.

"Awww!" Martha did not give up that easily. "You know nobody makes peanut brittle like Mr. Doyle. He puts in so many more peanuts, for one thing."

"You've guessed my secret," he said, watching Ellen.

A woman flipping through magazines while her husband chose ice cream put down the new *Maclean's*.

"You mean that's homemade candy?" she demanded, coming to the counter.

Mr. Doyle stopped smiling.

"Candy-making's my hobby," he told her. "Every

so often, I make up a batch for customers like Martha. Martha has the biggest sweet tooth in the Province of Ontario."

Martha grinned, not minding his teasing. She did not like the way the woman was eyeing the peanut brittle, however.

"Sam, how about some candy?" She summoned her husband.

Sam, a tall, gangly man, drifted over.

"I always have been partial to peanut brittle," he said.

"Ellen!" Martha's voice was outraged.

"Okay," Ellen said. "We'll take half a pound."

"A pound," Martha corrected. "We have company."

"One pound it is," Mr. Doyle agreed, taking the candy out. "Well, it's a couple of ounces over—but I'll throw that in for free, seeing as how you've broken your arm and all."

Martha turned to Sam, who was looking disappointed.

"His fudge is very good," Martha said, "and the Turkish delight is . . . delightful."

She giggled at her own wit. Sam smiled too.

"Now wait just a moment, young lady," his wife started in angrily.

"Easy," Mr. Doyle interrupted. "I have more peanut brittle out back for Sam. You paying for this, Martha?"

Chadron State College Library
Chadron, Nebraska

"Me?" Martha looked indignant. "I do not pay for groceries. I am poverty-stricken."

Ellen paid. Kit stood back, clearly wishing Martha would be quieter.

"Thanks, Mr. Doyle." Ellen hoisted the bags of groceries up into her arms. " 'Bye."

The girls started filing out. Sam's wife snapped, "Where's the peanut brittle?" but Mr. Doyle ignored her. He was still watching Martha. Kit started to follow Rosemary, but Martha caught at her arm.

"Wait." Then turning to the storekeeper, she said, "I'll have a loaf of bread, please."

"I thought you never paid for groceries," Sam said as Martha fished coins out of her pocket.

Kit squirmed. She'll call him Sam any minute now, she thought.

"This isn't exactly groceries, Sam," Martha explained. "I'd tell you about it, but I want to surprise Kit. Ask Mr. Doyle after we go. He knows."

"Sam, we haven't all day," his wife said.

"Sure we do, Maisie. We're on vacation," Sam answered.

Mr. Doyle slid the bread across the counter and scooped up the change.

"Now, which will you have first, Samuel, an explanation or your candy?" he asked as the girls left.

The wind had stiffened. The waves were darker

now and they were real waves, although there were no whitecaps yet. Kit eyed them and then turned quickly to Martha to ask about the bread.

Martha was gone.

For an instant, Kit just stood there staring after her.

Martha was bounding down the beach like an antelope. She held her broken arm close against her chest as she ran, and without noticing mashed the loaf of bread under her other elbow. The magic of sun and wind captured Kit too then, and she took off after Martha. It was a day especially created for running. The two girls passed Ellen and Rosemary in no time.

"Christine, where are you going?" Rosemary shouted after them.

Kit kept running. Suddenly Martha stopped. Using her good hand and the fingers of her other one, she tore open the bread wrapper and took out the top slice. Then she threw it high in the air. At once a seagull dove and caught it in his beak. Then he skimmed away with two others chasing him.

"Ohhhh, Marth!" Kit cried.

"Wait," Martha told her. "You haven't seen anything yet. Stand still."

Kit froze. Martha threw another slice and then another. Then she held one up in her fingers, as high above her head as she could. Gulls circled, swooped, soared up again and screamed at her to throw it. Martha stood her ground and waited. Finally a fat, brazen gull swept lower than the others had dared to and snatched it from her hand.

"Now," Martha said—and handed Kit a slice.

Rosemary and Ellen caught up to them. They put down the groceries and stood watching. Kit held the bread up high. The gulls went around and around. They would not come to her.

"Throw them part of it first," Martha advised. "They don't know you yet."

Kit tossed half the slice above her head. Two gulls caught it at once and fought fiercely over it. Between them, they dropped it and a third, smaller bird grabbed it as it fell.

Kit tried again, holding the bread and waiting.

Swish! She felt the beat of wings. A shadow came over her. She cringed but before she could be frightened, the bread was gone.

Kit looked at her own hand in wonder. It looked the same as always, but it felt new, strange. She turned eagerly to Martha.

"Give me some more."

Martha handed over two more slices. Then she saw Rosemary's face. Her eyes were full of longing. Her hair, streaming in the wind, was more tangled than Kit's could ever be.

The gulls had changed Kit. She was no longer

closed in and silent, but openly excited. Like a new person. Why shouldn't Rosemary have a chance to change?

Martha smiled at her and handed her a slice too.

Rosemary smiled back, and then went up on her toes and held her hand high to tempt a gull to her.

Soon the whole loaf was gone. The gulls, seeing Martha reach down and crumple the empty wrapper, rose in a great squabbling flock and departed.

"They are the greediest birds on earth," Ellen said, looking after them.

"Oh, but they're lovely to look at!" Rosemary defended them.

Martha agreed. Their wings looked brushed with silver as the sunlight caught them. They coasted on nothing, mounted, dipped. One of them screeched and they all turned and flew out over the lake.

"They really ought to sing," Kit said.

Ellen picked up one bag of groceries, Rosemary the other. They started ahead. Kit fell in beside Martha. Martha, heading for home, was quiet. She had fed those gulls all last summer until they came zooming down to her each time she came out of the store. And now she had shared them with Kit, had even given her the bread and shown her what to do so that, in a few minutes, Kit had done what had taken Martha days.

I'm glad I did, she told herself, angry at her feeling of loss.

106

Then, in her mind's eye, she saw Kit as the gull took the bread from her hand, and she really was glad. Kit's face had been so bright with happiness when she had stopped being scared.

When they got home, there was not much left of the morning. They fiddled away the time till lunch.

"Let's swim," Martha suggested afterward.

"It's beginning to get rough," Ellen said, looking out at the lake. Kit looked too, but the sky was as blue as ever.

"It's gorgeous out," Martha maintained. "And tomorrow it probably will be really rough and we won't be able to go in. Come on, dumdum," she ordered. "Come ON!"

Soon she and Kit were crossing the beach to the lake's edge. The others followed more slowly.

"Let's run in, Kit!" Martha shouted as they neared the water.

"Martha, be careful of your arm," Ellen called after her.

"I'm okay," Martha called, and she led the way. Where Martha led, Kit did her best to follow. They tore into the shallow water, taking great leaping strides, splashing wildly. Then at the same instant, they toppled forward into the water.

Martha did fall awkwardly and her arm twinged, but the sling held it safely and she was laughing when she struggled to her knees. Kit, nearby, shook the water out of her eyes and laughed too. Then she stood up, bracing herself against the buffeting waves, and helped Martha to her feet.

"Boy, is it cold!" Martha exclaimed.

They headed out to deeper water. That morning, when they had gone in for their early dip, neither of them had done any real swimming. When they were up to their waists, Martha turned to Kit.

"Are you a really good swimmer?" she asked.

Kit did not answer. "What happened to your arm when you went under like that?" she asked instead.

"Nothing," Martha told her. "The sling keeps it bent. Besides, I can look after myself."

Kit smiled. Then she struck out in a smooth, speedy crawl. Martha gasped and then swam after her. Even without a broken arm, Martha did not swim expertly like Kit. She fought the water, sending up showers of spray, bobbing up for air every few seconds, and rolling like a porpoise, only with less grace. She tried hard, but she did not make much headway. Every time she surfaced, she saw Kit, still ahead of her, cutting cleanly through the water.

Martha finally put her feet down and waited. The water was deeper now and the waves, when they came, slapped as high as her chin. If she went any farther, she would be out of her depth. She would be safe enough, even if she did go deeper, she told herself, but it was nice to know the bottom was right there when you got tired.

At last, Kit was on her way back. As far as Martha could tell, she had not put her feet down yet.

So the mouse is a great swimmer, so what? Martha asked the blue sky.

Until that instant, she had not realized that Kit sometimes reminded her of a mouse. Especially when Rosemary was nagging at her.

Then Kit disappeared.

Martha stared at the spot where she had last seen her. What did you do when somebody just sank out of sight? Was Kit drowning? Why didn't she come up and call for help? Martha turned to yell for Ellen. The other two girls were still on the beach. Ellen was putting suntan lotion on Rosemary's back. Would they hear above the noise of the water?

"Ellen!" Martha shouted.

Two small strong hands clutched her ankles and tugged her feet out from under her. Martha, her mouth still wide open, went under with a swoosh. Spluttering, choking with laughter, surprise and a mouthful of Lake Huron, she made it back to the surface. Kit bobbed up beside her, grinning uncertainly. She tossed back her wet hair.

"Don't call me a dumdum," she said, and waited for Martha to explode.

"Wow! That was something!" Martha panted. "Where'd you learn to swim like that? How can you stay under so long?"

"It's easy," Kit said. "I learned at . . . uh . . . camp."

Martha heard the small hesitation and understood it.

"Did I hurt you?" Kit asked quickly.

Martha shook her head. Kit was getting mouselike again.

"Hey, look at Ellen!" Martha ordered in an excited voice.

Kit turned and Martha plunged into the water like some big blundering whale. She could not make it anywhere near Kit's feet, and she only had one arm free for attack. But Kit was small and thin. Martha tackled her around the waist and the two of them went down into the sparkling green-blue waves with a tremendous thrashing of legs.

"Why, you . . . you . . ." Kit came up snorting threats, water streaming off her.

"You asked for it," laughed Martha. "I wish you could teach me to swim like that."

"But how can you, with your arm?" Kit asked.

Martha looked glum. That last struggle to dunk Kit had been really hard with the sling in the way.

Then Rosemary and Ellen were there, and she stopped worrying about it.

"Let's play tag," she challenged.

"Tag!" Rosemary said, as though she was so old she had forgotten what the word meant.

Kit turned away.

110

Ellen said, "But Martha, your arm . . ."

Martha could not stand it. With a yell, she flung herself through the water at Rosemary. Rosemary, wide-eyed, watched her come. Martha raised her good hand and brought it down on Rosemary's shoulder with a wet smack.

"What . . . ?" Rosemary started indignantly.

"You're IT!" Martha shouted.

Kit looked startled. Ellen started to protest. But Rosemary laughed. She took two quick strokes and reached Ellen.

"No, I'm not," she called to Martha. "Ellen is!"

The game was on.

9 | The Trouble with Rosemary

"Christine, don't track in sand," Rosemary called as Kit and Martha, who had run ahead, were about to enter the cottage.

"I'm not!" Kit said, just loud enough for Martha to hear. Then, where Rosemary could see her, she stooped and brushed off her bare feet with her hand.

When they were in their room, Martha shut the door.

"What is this thing between you and Rosemary anyway?" she asked.

"What thing?" Kit stalled, climbing into her shorts.

Martha, still in her damp bathing suit, sat down on the edge of her bed and concentrated on the conversation.

"You know what thing. She's always after you about little things and you never say anything back. And she calls you Christine, never Kit. You don't act like sisters at all."

"I suppose you and Ellen never fight," Kit flared.

"Sure we do. Lots of times," Martha said. "But you and Rosemary don't. She nags and you . . . you act like a mouse. What I can't figure out is why."

"I do not. . . ." Kit said, and stopped. Martha, horrified, saw she had tears in her eyes.

"Oh, forget it," she said. "It's none of my business. I'm sorry I said anything."

Kit blinked the tears away and pulled on her shirt. Then, with a small tired sigh, she sank down on the bed opposite Martha.

"It's hard to explain," she said, spreading her fingers out like a fan and looking at them as though she hoped to see the answer there. "Part of it is just that she's furious at Dad for saying she had to come on this trip instead of going to Nancy's. When Rosemary's mad, she stays mad for ages and she has to take it out on somebody. Seeing Dad isn't around, I'm elected."

"But you didn't have anything to do with it, did you?"

"No. But I'm Dad's favorite so she knows I'm on his side."

"You mean your father says right out that you're his favorite?" Martha could not believe it.

"Not in those words, maybe, but we both know. It's only fair when Mother likes Rosemary so much more," Kit said.

Martha let herself collapse backward onto the bed and stared up at the rafters. She had no idea what to say next. Kit sounded so calm, as if what she was saying was perfectly ordinary.

"What's come over you?" Kit's puzzled voice

brought Martha back up to a sitting position. "Don't your parents have favorites?"

"I don't think so. They say they don't and if they do, we can't tell," Martha said.

There was a short awkward silence. Then Kit, whom Martha had just finished calling a mouse, glared at Martha and burst out with a torrent of defiant words.

"Well, our family's different, that's all. Rosemary and Mother like all the same things so why shouldn't they get along better? They can talk about clothes for hours. Mother's proud of Rosemary because she's so poised. But I don't care if I DON'T have poise. Dad likes me just the way I am. When he's home, we talk about books and go on walks and lots of things. I just wish he was home more, that's all."

Kit choked on a sob and stopped. This time she could not keep the tears back.

"Don't," Martha said, getting up and standing beside her. "Please don't cry. I didn't mean to make you feel bad."

One more minute and she'd be bawling too, Martha knew. But Kit gulped, sniffed, snatched up a Kleenex from the bedside table and mopped her face —and it was over.

"I'm okay," she said. "Go on and get dressed."

Martha, her head whirling with everything Kit had blurted out, went to where her clothes lay in a heap and began turning her shorts right side out.

114

She realized she still did not know why Kit would not stick up for herself when Rosemary was mean to her, but she certainly was not going to ask again.

"With Ellen for a sister, you just would never understand," Kit said behind her. "You two even share a room. Rosemary would die if she had to share a room with me. She thinks everything I do is wrong."

Martha forgot she was going to change the subject.

"Why don't you stand up for yourself?" she demanded, whirling to face Kit. "Fight back!"

"What's the use? She's just copying Mother."

Kit's voice dragged. Her face, still marked with tears, looked sullen and defeated. Suddenly Martha felt less sorry for her.

She sulks, she thought. And she's a crybaby. No wonder Rosemary picks on her.

Then she felt ashamed. Kit had not been faking those tears. On the other hand, Rosemary had loved feeding the gulls and had been lots of fun when they had played water tag. So she was not simply a bully although sometimes, most of the time even, she acted like it.

Kit, while she waited, had wandered over to the boys' bookcase and was glancing over the titles.

"Your brothers sure must be crazy about Indians," she said. "There's almost a whole shelf of books about them here."

115

Martha did up her zipper.

"They should be," she said idly. "Their father was one."

"What?" Kit said.

Martha looked up at her.

"Didn't you know they're adopted?" she asked.

"Adopted!" Kit sounded as though she had never heard the word before.

"Sure. We've only had them for two years. Bruce's seven and Toby's five."

Kit thought back to the hour or so she had spent in Bruce and Toby's company.

"They don't look Indian," she said.

Martha was down on her knees, pulling a box out from under her bed.

"Well, they aren't exactly. I guess they look more like their mother. I look like one of my aunts. She's fat too."

"Go on," Kit prompted when Martha stopped.

"Go on about what?" Martha was busy poking into the box.

"Go on about Bruce and Toby."

Martha sat up, cross-legged, and paid proper attention. "Well, they're brats, but when they first came they were a lot worse. Bruce cried an awful lot. His mother used to beat him up. Toby was still little and cute so she made a pet out of him. Bruce used to have nightmares and wake us all up but he

116

hardly ever has one now. Toby was a real little devil right from the start."

Kit sank down on her bed. She linked her hands behind her head and gazed off into space.

"I wish I had brothers," she said.

"You wouldn't if you had them," Martha said. "Hey, Kit, close your eyes for a second."

"Why?" Kit asked, still preoccupied.

"Just because," Martha said. "Go on."

Kit let her eyes close. She felt something land on her chest, something very light. Then it moved and she opened her eyes, without waiting for Martha to say she could. Henrietta, Martha's hairy rubber spider, was about to twitch her way up onto Kit's chin.

Kit shrieked and leaped up. Martha collapsed giggling on the floor between the beds. Kit jumped on her. Not worrying about Martha's injured arm, she shook her as hard as she could. Kit being Kit and Martha being Martha, she did not move her much, but Martha got the idea.

"Quit! I surrender!" she said. "Isn't she a great spider though? Watch her walk."

"Not on me," Kit said.

"Of course not," Martha assured her. "That was just a test."

Kit turned Henrietta over onto her back and then jerked her string so that all her legs waved in the air.

117

"What sort of a test?" she asked.

Martha hesitated.

"A test to see if you were really a mouse," she said then.

Kit looked up, her eyes sparking into anger.

"Don't get excited," Martha said. "You aren't. You just act like one sometimes, I guess. Look at my other stuff."

Kit started to splutter, but then she glimpsed the tricks stowed away in Martha's box. For the next hour, they fooled around with them happily.

"Which one shall we use on Rosemary?" Martha asked slyly at last.

Kit grinned and then quickly sobered.

"I don't want to get her madder," she said, not looking at Martha. "*You* could do it though. Maybe just before we leave."

Martha sighed. She still had a lot of work to do on Kit; she could see that.

For supper, they had Kraft Dinner and cold ham and salad.

"What happened to the pork chops?" asked Martha.

"We're having them tomorrow," Ellen said.

There was a sharp edge to her voice. Kit was watching.

She's hoping Ellen and I will have a fight, Martha thought.

She grinned at Ellen.

"Okay," she said amiably. "Just so we have them."

Ellen sighed, but said nothing more.

After supper, they played Scrabble. Martha and Kit were both hopelessly behind.

"Let's see what letters you have, Christine," Rosemary said, turning Kit's holder around so she could scan them.

"Why, look," she said a moment later. "You can play Q-U-E-S-T. Quest. And on a double letter score. That's very good."

Kit allowed Rosemary to place the letters for her.

"That's cheating," Martha said too loudly. "Kit should play her own."

"She just needed a little help," Rosemary said. "I'll help you too if you like."

"I can play my own letters just fine, thank you," Martha said.

She looked and looked at the line of letters in front of her. V, R, C, K, U, W and another V. She could not see a thing she could play.

"Come on, Martha. We can't wait all night," Ellen said.

Rosemary looked down at her own letters. Martha was sure she was smiling. Grimly, she made Cut. There were no extra points for playing in the right place. After Kit's score, hers was hardly worth totaling.

"I'm tired," she said, a couple of turns later. "You finish. I'm going to bed."

"Me too," Kit said quickly.

Martha ignored her. She waited for Ellen to agree. Ellen was peering at the board. She suddenly cried, "I can. I CAN!"

Using Martha's C, she played Chicken on a triple word score.

"Okay, Marth," she said, busy counting. "Sleep tight."

"Good night, girls," Rosemary said as they headed for the stairs.

She talks to us as though we're Toby's age, Martha fumed.

She did not share her thoughts with Kit, however. Kit had let Rosemary boss her around again and Martha was fed up with her. They got ready for bed in silence. But it was too early to go to sleep.

"Would you like a book to read?" Martha demanded ungraciously.

"No, thank you," Kit said in her mousiest voice. "I haven't finished *Warrior Scarlet* yet."

Martha went to the bookcase she shared with Ellen, put back *The Secret Language* and finally settled on *My Friend Flicka*. She came back, got into bed without a word and bent her head over the book.

But she could not keep her mind on it. Instead she listened to the wind worrying the house, blustering about like the Big Bad Wolf. Tomorrow ought to be a wonderful wild day.

120

But how could she look forward to it properly? What was the use of a Blow to roam around in if all you had for company was a mouse?

Kit closed her book with a little bang.

"I'm going to sleep," she said.

Martha pretended to finish the page. Then she too switched off her light.

To think she had once dreamed staying here might be like being at camp! Camp Better-Than-Nothing.

It isn't, Martha thought. It's WORSE!

"Kit," she said into the darkness, "what are you thinking about?"

"The gulls," Kit said. "That was so wonderful, Marth."

Martha's bad temper evaporated.

"We'll feed them again tomorrow," she promised.

10 | Gin Rummy

In the morning, the wind was too strong for them to go into the water.

"We're going to the store," Martha announced after breakfast. "Give me some money, Ellen, and I'll buy more peanut brittle."

"You bring every bit of it home, then," Ellen said. "Honestly, I was ashamed last night when I went to give Rosemary a piece and found the whole bowlful gone."

"Okay, okay," Martha agreed.

The gulls came, in spite of the wind, but it was harder for them to take the bread right from the girls' hands. Kit and Martha tossed most of it up for them to snatch out of the air.

"See, I told you a Blow was great," Martha said as they made their way home, leaning into the wind.

"This is okay," Kit said. "I mean, there's nothing to hurt you."

Martha smiled. Kit was not even thinking of hiding. Rosemary was nuts.

Then in early afternoon, great clouds began to

roll up over the horizon and blow across the sun. The waves, crested with foam, towered. Gusts of rain spattered the cottage, rattling against the glass doors, and, as suddenly as they came, blew away.

"We can't go out in this," Ellen said. "Let's play something."

Martha was torn. She loved going out into the wild weather, but she did like playing games too. Not stupid Scrabble, but good games. She looked out the window. The Blow was not yet at its height. She could play first and go out after.

"Monopoly," she suggested hopefully. It was her favorite game.

"That takes forever and you hardly ever finish. How about gin rummy?" Ellen said.

Next to Monopoly, Martha liked gin rummy best. She nodded.

"But only two people can play gin rummy," Rosemary objected.

Trust Rosemary! Martha gave her a pitying look.

"We have our own rules," she said. "You'll see. It works fine."

Rosemary turned to her sister. "Christine hasn't played many card games," she said. "I play with the other kids, but she doesn't know a thing about cards, do you?"

"Not m-much," Kit agreed, head down.

Martha glared at her. Not again! Where was the joyous gull feeder, the sand-castle builder, the girl who had run in the sun with her and later dunked her in the lake?

Then, looking at Kit's unhappy face, she felt sorry. Kit probably did not plan to turn into a baby, but just could not help herself. It was a bad habit like nail-biting.

"I can teach you to play gin rummy," Martha said to her.

Hearing the warmth in Martha's voice, Kit lifted her head. She stopped being poor little Christine.

"Thanks, Martha," she said, not stammering at all.

"You teach her, Marth, and Rosemary and I'll play cribbage while she learns," Ellen planned for everyone. "It's too confusing learning from three teachers."

Ellen must have noticed what Rosemary does to Kit too, Martha guessed.

She and Kit sat down at the card table. Ellen and Rosemary went to the dining area. Martha picked up the cards. She had played various card games since she was six or seven, but now, with one arm in a sling, she found she could not shuffle. Even holding the cards was not easy.

"You shuffle," she told Kit.

"I'm no good at it," Kit protested.

"You can't help but be better than I am right now," Martha said.

Kit dropped a lot of cards in the process, but she

did manage to shuffle the deck and deal as Martha directed. She was a good student too. She listened and asked questions when she was mixed up.

"And the twos are wild," Martha finished. "You can use them to fill in for any other missing card." She made a set of fives with one five not there and put a two in to take its place.

Kit nodded.

"Okay. Here we go," Martha said. "We won't count this first game so don't worry about losing. It'll just be practice."

Kit won.

"That's what they call beginner's luck," Martha said. "Your turn to go first."

Kit won the next two games.

"Ellen!" Martha yelled, although Ellen was just across the room. "We're ready to play with you now."

"Okay. We'll be right there when we finish this game," Ellen answered.

Martha, waiting, sat slumped in her chair. She kept cutting the deck, turning up the top few cards for no good reason. The older girls put away the cribbage board.

"I won," Ellen announced, seating herself next to Martha. "Both times."

Martha waited for Kit to brag too, but Kit just sat.

"It's high time we showed these two that Swanns

can also win," Rosemary said to Kit. "Just you watch me."

Martha started to say that Kit had showed her quite enough for one afternoon, but she caught Kit's eye and was silent. Kit must be hoping to surprise her sister.

I hope she does, too, Martha told herself. She hooked her bare toes together and made a wish for Kit's victory.

Martha ran through the Winston rules for gin rummy. Ellen dealt. Martha was proud of the way the cards seemed to leap from her sister's hands so swiftly, so neatly, landing exactly where she aimed them.

I bet Rosemary can't do it like that, she thought.

She stole a sideways look at Kit, but her face was half hidden by her hair.

Win, Martha thought at her. Win, win, win!

But Ellen won the first hand.

Martha added up the score. She was in the minuses. To cheer herself up, she looked at Rosemary to see how she liked being beaten. Rosemary looked fine. Not extra grown-up or bossy. Just the way anybody looked when she got caught with a lot of points against her.

"Never mind, Christine," Rosemary said then. "I'll fix them this next time."

Quit calling her Christine, Martha yelled inside her head.

Then something worked—either her good teaching or her linked toes. Kit won the next hand so fast that the other three were all caught with fists full of cards. Rosemary stared at her younger sister.

"They call that beginner's luck," she said.

Martha blushed faintly and sent a private grin in Kit's direction. Kit's face remained blank. Martha reached over with her toe and nudged Kit's ankle. But Kit did not smile. She handed her cards to Ellen to shuffle and then darted a look over her shoulder at the cottage window.

Ellen followed her glance.

"It's blowing up quite a gale," she said.

"Maybe it'll be a hurricane," Martha hoped. "That'd be great!"

Kit gasped.

"Let's play," Rosemary said quickly, eyeing her sister's tense face.

Martha hesitated. The card game was beginning to seem poky when she could be outside. Well, one more hand.

Before beginning, though, she unhooked her toes. Enough was enough. Her hand looked promising. She picked up a card. Why, if she got the right one next time, she could go out—and there were several possible right cards. Rosemary picked up, made a face, and discarded. Ellen played a set of three fives. But Kit was the one Martha was watching.

Kit simply picked up a card mechanically, scarcely glanced at her hand, and discarded. She must be really losing. She must have an impossible hand. She was still holding a lot of cards.

Martha's hand darted out and picked up the top card. The very one she had wanted most.

"I'm going out right now!" she said exultantly and played down her cards.

The others displayed their hands. Martha leaned over sympathetically to view those Kit was stuck with. Her eyes widened.

"But . . . but you could have played those. You could have gone out before I did!" she said incredulously.

Kit gave a quick shiver, stared at her cards and then nodded like a puppet.

"I didn't notice," she said in a flat voice.

Martha stared at her. Had Kit let her win on purpose? No, because she would not have known Martha could have won on that turn.

Before Martha could get it figured out, Rosemary jumbled her cards together in an untidy little heap and pushed them into the middle of the table.

"I'm sick of this," she said. "Let's do something else."

Ellen got to her feet. She stood erect, like a soldier going on guard duty.

"I have to get supper," she said.

"I did win that last hand," Martha stated. But it was hard to feel triumphant knowing Kit could have beaten her if she had been paying attention.

Suddenly she was startled to find Kit was all attention again. The others deserting the game seemed to have shocked her into new life. She scooped the cards towards her and tried to make them into a neat pile.

"We can still play, Martha," she said.

She sounded determined, almost desperate, as though she could not bear to stop. Martha felt bewildered. But one thing she was certain of. She did not want to play any more gin rummy.

"Let's not," she said. "It's getting nice outside now and it's downright stuffy in here."

Kit ignored Martha's words and began to shuffle the deck. Four cards slithered out of her grasp. Martha, feeling doomed, reached out and returned them.

Rosemary stood behind Kit's chair and watched.

"Want me to do that for you, Christine?" she asked.

Automatically Kit began to hand over the cards. She caught Martha's look of unbelief. At the last moment, she held on to them.

"I can do it," she mumbled—and dropped half the deck.

Martha saw her face was pale.

"You made her do that," she blazed at Rosemary. "She was doing fine before you said anything. I thought you said you didn't want to play."

Rosemary stared at Martha's angry face, at Kit's down-bent head. Then she said meekly, "I guess I'll go help Ellen. I didn't know I was butting in."

130

Kit started dealing. She hurried so that, when the cards hit the table, they skidded wildly. Then Martha saw that Kit's hands were actually shaking. Was standing up to Rosemary that hard on her?

"Calm down. She's gone," Martha said.

Again Kit made no response. She picked up the cards and gripped them so tightly that they bent in her hands.

"Who goes first?" she demanded. Her voice was shrill and it too shook.

Martha left her hand where it lay on the table, and stared at her friend.

"Hey, what's wrong with you?" she asked bluntly.

And Kit, almost against her own will, sent one more glance over her shoulder at the glass doors.

11 | Standing in the Wind

Then Martha saw what was going on in the world outside. At last everything had gone wild. The wind thudded against the house in huge boisterous gusts. Sudden bursts of rain rattled against the window panes. It was perfect.

Who cared about gin rummy?

She jumped to her feet.

"Come on," she urged a now cowering Kit. "Let's go outside."

"Outside?" Kit echoed as though Martha had said something insane.

"Sure. It's great on a day like this. Ellen, we're going out," she called.

"Okay," Ellen answered from the kitchen. She sounded absentminded.

Martha reached the door, started to tug it open and turned her head. Kit was still sitting hunched by the card table.

"It . . . it's raining," she said.

"So what? You're waterproof," Martha returned.

Tired of wasting time, she ran back and grabbed

Kit's hand. Before Kit could resist, Martha had dragged her to the door. Kit tried desperately to hang back, but Martha was so much stronger that the smaller girl did not have a chance.

"Oh, don't," Kit moaned. "It's a hurricane."

Martha was paying no attention. Letting go of Kit for a second, she raced back and snatched up a fistful of peanut brittle which Ellen had put in a bowl on the card table.

"We'll need this to keep us alive till supper," she said, stowing it in the pocket her mother had finally been persuaded to sew onto her shorts. Martha hated being without a pocket. Then she was back to where Kit was still standing like a hypnotized rabbit.

"It's pouring, Martha. It's awful out there," she cried as Martha returned to her.

As she spoke, however, the rain stopped abruptly and a shaft of sunlight gleamed across the tumult of water, the wet sand, and then swept in to include the two of them.

"See?" Martha tugged at her. "It's gorgeous. You'll find out. Hurry!"

Kit had no choice.

"Open the door," Martha ordered. She knew it would take two hands. Instantly the wind caught it and blew it shut again with a slam that made the glass rattle. Martha helped the next time, putting her strong hand over Kit's, and between them, they shoved the door wide again. Before Kit could get

133

her to stop and listen to her frantic pleas, Martha had pulled her out onto the windswept beach.

At once the gale roared at them, pried Kit loose and hurled her down the sand, away from Martha. Rain blew in a gust after her.

"Whee!" Martha howled as though it were all a great game.

Then she dashed after Kit and caught her. Kit clutched at her in real desperation.

"Oh, please, let's go in," she begged. "Please, please! We'll be killed!"

Martha, her hair standing straight up, her eyes shining, stared at the smaller girl clinging to her. Suddenly she again remembered Rosemary's words about Kit hiding in her closet when a storm came. She had taken it for granted that meant a thunder-and-lightning storm, but one glance showed her that Kit was honestly gripped by sheer terror at this very moment. It made no sense at all. Then she heard again Kit's voice bleating, "It's a hurricane. . . ."

People were sometimes killed in hurricanes. But heck! this was no hurricane. This was just a regular Big Blow.

"Killed?" Martha scoffed. "Killed by what? It's only the wind."

"Martha, please," Kit whimpered. "Please. I'm so scared."

For an instant, Martha took pity. Already they had been carried a hundred feet down the beach, but now she started battling their way back against the storm, towing Kit to safety.

Except we ARE safe, Martha thought, and stopped dead in her tracks. Not loosening her grip on the now weeping Kit, she did her best to think in the middle of the noise and excitement.

"Kit, KIT!" she shouted, at last, right into Kit's ear.

"What?" Kit sobbed, her voice nearly blown away.

"Will you try something?"

"I want to go home," Kit insisted.

"I'll take you home if you'll do me a favor first," Martha bargained.

Kit was obviously ready to promise anything that would bring rescue. She nodded.

Martha knew somehow she had to get Kit to stop shaking long enough to notice the glory of the wild bluster around them. The clouds raced across the sky, great curly ones, dark grey and white jumbled and heaped together. Rain pelted down; then the sun speared through. Thundering waves reared up and flung themselves about.

Martha reached into her pocket.

"If you stand up and look out at the lake and eat this whole piece of peanut brittle without moving, I'll take you back to the cottage," she promised.

"Eat . . . !" Kit looked dazed. Her hair was flattened and drenched. If she looked like a mouse now, it was a half-drowned one. But Martha did not let herself relent.

"Come on. One piece of candy. That's all."

She let go of Kit, and Kit immediately stumbled away, carried along by a great push of wind.

"Stand up to it," Martha shrieked at her, dragging her back. "Look. Put your feet apart. Like this. That's it. Now lean into the wind. Stand! You'll never love it if you let it shove you around."

"Stand," Kit repeated.

She did not seem to be taking in what Martha said. But suddenly she was doing it. Small as she was, she was facing the wind, bracing her feet. It was trying to sweep her away, but she was stronger.

"Here!" Martha pushed the piece of peanut brittle into Kit's hand.

Kit's fingers closed over it. She got it into her mouth and crunched.

"See?" Martha encouraged. Jumping up and down, she now lost her balance and toppled to the sand. Kit was horrified. But Martha, sling awry, just sat there for an instant, laughing, and then fought her way back onto her two feet. She jammed candy into her own mouth and stood there, eating it and somehow smiling at the same time.

Then, astonishing Kit yet again, Martha began to sing.

The words were not clear at first. They were all mixed up with the roaring of the gale, and besides,

Martha's mouth was full. But then, in a brief lull, they sounded out. Martha was chanting to the tune of "Here we go gathering nuts in May":

I stand in the wind and eat peanut brittle!
I stand in the wind and eat peanut brittle!

"Martha, you're crazy," Kit cried.

"Try it," Martha called back, grabbing her hand.

Then Kit too sang the ridiculous words: "I stand in the wind and eat peanut brittle!"

She heard Martha say something and turned her head.

"What did you say?" she asked.

Martha, drenched and very happy, repeated her question.

"I said, 'Are you still scared?'"

"Of course I am," Kit started. Then she admitted, "No, I guess not. What is there to be scared of?"

Martha looked even more pleased with herself.

"I stand in the wind and eat peanut brittle!" Kit yelled, not bothering to sing.

"Okay, okay," Martha laughed. "We'd better go home or we'll never get changed in time to eat. I'm starving."

She seemed to have forgotten the peanut brittle she had just consumed. Arms linked, they struggled with the wind, making their way back up the beach.

"I love it," Kit said, tossing her wet hair back and

looking up at the tumbling clouds with the sudden patches of blue between them.

"Sure," Martha agreed. "Who wouldn't?"

They reached the cottage door. Kit opened it. They stumbled in, dripping, out of breath, triumphant.

"I was so terrified," Kit marveled as they headed for the stairs, leaving a trail of sandy, wet footprints behind them. "It must have been the peanut brittle."

She laughed as she said it, and waited for Martha, ahead of her on the stairs, to laugh too. Martha ran to the top and then turned. Her face was serious, as though she had just found out something important.

"No," she said, searching for words. "It was just standing there really. You have to stand in the wind . . ." She hesitated.

Kit was still laughing. "And eat peanut brittle," she finished.

"Hurry up, you goon," Martha said, the seriousness gone as swiftly as it had come. "I'm starved. And not for peanut brittle either. I want my pork chop."

12 | Pork Chops

Martha pulled off her sopping clothes and rummaged in the dresser for something dry. Moving gingerly, she switched slings. Kit located a dry outfit before she began to change.

"Here's a towel for your hair," Martha said.

Smothered in the towel, Kit missed what Martha said next.

"Pardon?" she asked, emerging.

"I was just wondering how supper was coming along."

Kit listened. "They're awfully quiet, aren't they? I don't hear pots and pans and stuff."

"Well, we were out for ages," Martha said. "They should be about ready. Only I don't smell any pork chops."

Kit sniffed.

"I do sort of," she said. "Faintly."

"Let's investigate," Martha said and headed for the stairs.

Rosemary barred their way before they reached the kitchen.

"We aren't ready yet," she told them. "Read a book or something for ten minutes."

"Rosemary! Rosemary!" Ellen called from the kitchen.

Martha did not miss the frantic note in that cry. "What's happening?" she said.

Rosemary gave her an icy look. "Sit down and WAIT!" She ran back to Ellen.

Martha and Kit sat down, though Martha muttered, "I can go where I please. It's MY house."

The next instant she was quiet, trying to overhear the conversation in the kitchen.

"We should never have boiled them," Ellen was saying. "I know Mother uses mushroom soup. Frying now isn't helping. They've shrunk!"

"Well, I only said I know sausages get boiled," Rosemary returned. Her voice dropped but was still audible. "The kids are out there waiting."

"Oh dear, I don't know what to do." Ellen tried to keep her voice down. "I wish Mother was home. Look at that cabbage!"

"Don't worry. They'll never notice," Rosemary murmured.

Kit and Martha exchanged glances. Martha made a face. Kit shook her head at her.

"I'm serving it up, for better or for worse," Rosemary announced. There was a pause, a clink of plates. Then she added, "Heavens, they're like rocks!"

Martha could not stand it. She started to get up.

"Martha, wait," Kit ordered.

It was so unlike her that Martha subsided for a moment. Then Rosemary appeared carrying two plates. Martha sprang up this time but Rosemary held the plates high.

"Take your places," she snapped. "Don't be pushy."

Before Martha could think of a squelching answer, Ellen followed with two more plates. Martha stared down at her dish.

"What is THAT?" she demanded.

Nobody answered. The answer was obvious. Dinner. But the pork chop for which Martha had been waiting so eagerly was tiny and wizened. The cabbage looked drowned. The potatoes were cold; the dabs of butter Rosemary had put on them were not melting at all. Only the peas seemed to have escaped disaster.

Grimly, Martha picked up her fork and jabbed it at her pork chop. It was rock hard. It skidded away, left her plate completely and landed halfway across the table.

Ellen, sinking onto her chair, stared blankly at the runaway chop. Rosemary glared at Martha.

"That is your pork chop," she said loudly.

She turned her fierce look on Kit.

Kit got the message. Cleverly, she began with the peas. They behaved well, going neatly into her mouth. But nobody was silencing Martha. She bit into a piece of potato and let out a yelp.

"It's as hard as a bullet," she accused. "And look at the cabbage! It's swimming in water. Ellen, this supper is horrible."

Ellen jumped up.

"Get your own supper then," she told her sister.

"I'll do just that," Martha returned. "I'll make myself a sandwich. Nobody could eat this yucky stuff!"

At that, Ellen ran from the room. Her feet clattered up the stairs. Her bedroom door banged shut. And, too late, Martha was sorry.

Rosemary let loose. "You revolting little beast!" she stormed. "It took her hours to get that supper ready!"

"Hours!" scoffed Martha. "You only started at five thirty. . . ."

"Never mind the time." Rosemary was on her feet now. "I'll bet you knew all along Ellen didn't know how to cook pork chops, but you had to go and embarrass her into buying them!"

Martha was in a rage but she had asked for those pork chops. Not for the cabbage, though. Or the raw potatoes!

"I didn't make her cook potatoes," she yelled. "That supper is only fit for pigs."

"Then you should love every bite of it," Rosemary shot back.

Kit had finished her peas and had come to a standstill, looking unhappily at the rest of the meal.

"Christine, you eat!" her big sister barked.

Kit took a forkful of potatoes but Martha reached out in the same instant almost and knocked it out of her hand.

"She doesn't have to eat that." She was as furious on Kit's behalf as Rosemary was on Ellen's. "I'll make her something decent."

"You couldn't cook a real supper if you tried!" Rosemary challenged with a sneer. "Peanut-butter sandwiches, that's your speed."

"I could cook a lot better meal than this any day of the week," Martha flung back, thrusting her plate so that it shot toward Rosemary, spilling peas as it went.

"All right. I dare you," Rosemary said, her voice suddenly deadly. "I'm going up to Ellen. Call us when you're ready. Let's see you put up or shut up."

"Okay. GO!" Martha shouted grandly.

Rosemary left with a swish.

Kit stared at Martha, whose face was as red as a lobster. Her eyes seemed to shoot off sparks of fury.

"Wh-what are . . . you . . . g-going to do?" Kit quavered.

"We," Martha said, stalking out to the kitchen, taking her plate with her, "are going to get a delicious dinner and show HER!"

"H-how?" Kit ventured.

There was silence in the kitchen. Then, still holding her dish, Martha returned, her face sheepish. She flopped down onto her chair.

"I haven't the foggiest idea," she said.

Kit looked at her woeful expression and her arm in its sling.

"Well," Kit said at last, "eat your peas while you think. They may be cold now but mine were good."

Martha looked startled. Then she reached for her fork, laughing suddenly at her own predicament and at the funny look on Kit's face. As though she had just seen a tiger turn into a toy kitten. Martha took one cautious bite.

"Not bad," she commented, and ate the peas.

13 | It's Just a Joke!

They went together to explore. Kit discovered a box of pancake mix in one of the cupboards. She grabbed it triumphantly.

"I know how to do pancakes," she cried. "We made them on sleep-outs."

"Sleep-outs!" Martha's present problems melted away for a moment. "You mean at camp, don't you? Tell me about them. What did you take? Where did you go?"

"Not now," Kit's soft voice was surprisingly stern. "We have to get supper. You told Rosemary, remember."

Martha had no trouble remembering. She sighed deeply. Kit puzzled over the instructions.

"Have you got a skillet?"

"We have a frying pan. It's there." Martha pointed at the debris Rosemary and Ellen had left behind. Kit looked and nodded.

"That's a skillet," she said, "but we'll have to wash it. I think they burned something in it."

"Yeah. My pork chop," mourned Martha.

146

"Forget it," Kit said. "We need milk and an egg. We'll make the specially rich ones. Find the syrup, too."

Martha found what Kit needed and then looked around again at the mess. Belatedly, Ellen's face was haunting her. Also, Ellen only ran away like that if she was going to cry. If she could clean up the kitchen, Martha thought Ellen might forgive her. She started trying to set things straight but she was soon defeated. It was hard to know where to begin and she only had one useful hand.

"Move so I can wash the skillet," Kit ordered.

Martha gladly backed away from the sink and watched Kit scour the frying pan till it shone.

The first pancakes Kit made, however, were disasters. She turned them too soon and they stuck. One burned. Another landed on the side of the pan when she tried to flip it. Kit's face reddened and her lips pressed tightly together. Martha stood by, silently sympathetic, but feeling helpless.

Kit opened the garbage can and threw that batch away. Martha finally saw a way to be useful. She reached up and opened the window above the sink so that the smoke would drift out and away before Rosemary came flying down to see what was burning. Kit ran water over the blackened pan. When it stopped hissing, she scoured it again, getting set for a fresh start.

"These are away better," she announced as she

flipped the first four neatly. "I forgot you had to wait for bubbles to come on top last time. Go and see if the table looks okay, Marth."

Martha rounded the table, clearing off everything left from the earlier meal including stray peas which had been spilled during her fight with Rosemary. She brought in the pitcher of maple syrup and a plate of butter. She even got a pitcher of ice water ready. By the time she was done, Kit had a pile of pancakes keeping warm in the oven. Martha stood still and looked at everything.

Only one thing was wrong.

It's too good for that Rosemary, Martha thought.

She stared at the table for a second longer. Then, quickly, she moved about, making her own arrangements.

Kit, bringing in the pancakes, caught her.

"What's that?"

"Never mind," Martha told her. "It's just a joke. It won't hurt."

"But, Martha, the supper's so nice. . . ."

"This won't change that, dopey. You'll see."

"I think Ellen was crying." Kit made one last appeal.

"Ellen can take a joke. It'll cheer her up," Martha insisted. "Don't worry. Hey, Ellen! Rosemary! Supper!" she called.

Kit bolted into the kitchen. Martha ran after her.

"Listen, if you mind that much I'll tell them right

now," she said. "But I'm always doing things to Ellen and she just laughs—after the first minute or so," she added.

"Pancakes!" they both heard Rosemary exclaim in delight.

"Martha?" Ellen asked.

"We'll be right there," Martha called back. She grabbed Kit by the elbow. "Come on then. I'll confess."

"Wait," Kit said, and stopped to undo her apron.

When they entered, Ellen was staring at everything on the table with a suspicious air. Something in Martha's voice must have alerted her. Rosemary was busy sloshing syrup over the biggest pancake.

"Ellen," Martha started in.

Ellen reached out, dipped a finger in the water, and tasted it.

"You salted it! I thought you'd done something," she cried. "Martha, you are awful."

Martha giggled.

"That's not all," she said, stepping forward. "Rosemary's found the other . . ."

She stopped and stared at Rosemary. Her eyes widened with shock. Kit looked too and gasped. Ellen looked from one to the other. Rosemary, still busy eating, glanced up.

"They're delicious," she said. "I apologize, Martha."

Martha did not smile.

"What did you do with the ointment?" she said.

Rosemary paused, her fork halfway to her mouth. "Ointment?" she echoed. "What are you talking about?"

"You couldn't have eaten it," Martha said weakly. "You COULDN'T have. It would taste horrible. I didn't try it but it smelled awful."

"Martha," Ellen snapped. "Tell me what you are babbling about right this INSTANT!"

Martha hung her head.

"I . . . we . . . no, it was me. Kit wouldn't . . ." she stammered.

Ellen appeared to be on the point of exploding. Rosemary was still bewildered. Kit took over. She did not stammer at all.

"You're just trying to make Martha feel bad, and that's mean," she accused. "She put that stuff for burns on the butter knife, but nobody would eat it. You'd notice the taste right away. It wasn't even the same color as butter."

There was a huge silence. Rosemary sat up stiffly.

"I took a lot of syrup," she said slowly. "I didn't notice a thing. I was so hungry."

"Where is the ointment?" Ellen's voice cut like a knife.

"On the kitchen counter," Martha said.

Ellen flew to the kitchen and returned with the tube of ointment in her hand.

"For burns, cuts, and minor abrasions . . ." she

150

read as she came in. She paused suddenly, and then
went on in horror.

WARNING: FOR EXTERNAL USE ONLY.
KEEP OUT OF REACH OF YOUNG CHILDREN.

Kit sniffled. Martha gave an audible gulp. She
wanted to run and hide, but she stood where she
was. Rosemary put one hand to her throat.

"It was only a little bit, wasn't it?" she asked
feebly.

Ellen dropped the ointment and turned on her
sister. "Well, Martha, you've really done it this
time," she announced. "You've probably poisoned
Rosemary."

At Ellen's words, Rosemary paled, Kit's sniffle became a sob, and Martha broke down completely.

"Oh, Ellen, I didn't mean to do it," she cried.
"I'll never do it again. Never!"

"You may not have the chance," Ellen said. "How
do you feel really, Rosemary?"

Rosemary was sitting up rigidly. She closed her
eyes. As the others watched, she began to sway.

"Rosemary, stop it!"

Ellen took two strides, grabbed Rosemary by the
back of her neck and thrust her head down between
her knees. When she let go, Rosemary came up, her
pallor gone, her expression a mixture of indignation,
surprise and relief.

151

"I feel fine," she said. "For a minute, I thought I was fainting, but . . ."

"You were just suffering from shock," Ellen said glibly, quoting her first-aid course at Guides.

Rosemary looked at Ellen with respect.

"You . . ." she started. Then she caught sight of Martha. Her eyes were enormous and she too was swaying dizzily.

"Look at Martha," Rosemary told Ellen.

Ellen whipped across the room, pushed her sister down on the nearest chair, and gave her the same treatment she had given Rosemary. As she did so, she studied Kit. Tears were trickling down Kit's cheeks, but otherwise she looked quite herself. She read Ellen's worried gaze correctly and smiled through the tears.

"I'm okay," she said. "If only Rosemary is . . ."

Her unfinished sentence hung in the air. Nobody needed to hear the rest. Martha squirmed, and Ellen let her sit up.

"How much did you put on the knife?" Ellen asked.

Martha sprang up, grabbed the tube and demonstrated.

"Just a tiny glob like that. Not hardly any really. I didn't want you to notice. Ohhhh!"

"Martha, stop falling apart and try being a help!" Ellen commanded.

"It's my own fault," Rosemary said, trying to comfort Martha. "I shouldn't have taken all that syrup." Her voice came out faint and saintly.

Martha looked more distraught than ever.

"Lie down, Rosemary," Kit said suddenly, startling them all. "Hurry up and lie down."

"I'll call Dad." Martha darted to the phone. "He'll know what to do."

In her anxiety, she did not even worry about what her father would have to say to her.

She held the receiver under her chin and dialed as quickly as she could. The telephone made no sound. "It's not ringing," she wailed, giving the receiver a shake.

"The line must have blown down," Ellen said. "It was dead when I tried using it to get advice about the pork chops."

"Well, let's go next door," Martha begged. "Let's not just sit and do nothing. I can't stand it."

She eyed Rosemary as she spoke. Any minute now she might go purple in the face and start choking. Martha knew about poisons. She had not been an avid TV fan for years for nothing. It would all be over in a matter of seconds if they did not get help.

"Dr. Hill," Ellen said suddenly. "I should have thought of him right away. If time's important, we should get her to someone who knows."

"His cottage is too far," Martha objected. Rosemary would never make it. They would end up with a body on the beach.

154

"No it isn't," said Ellen. She turned to Rosemary. "How do you feel now?"

"I don't feel a thing wrong," Rosemary stood up with care. "A little sort of pain . . . but maybe I just ate too fast."

Kit and Martha exchanged terrified looks.

Five more minutes and I'm a murderer, Martha told herself.

"Come on," Ellen spoke sharply. "We're leaving."

She pulled open the door.

"Ooooh!" Kit gasped as the night, wilder than ever, rushed in and pelted Ellen with rain.

Martha forgot Rosemary for a second. She ran to the table and grabbed one last piece of peanut brittle from the candy dish.

"Here," she said, thrusting it into Kit's hand. "Nothing's different from before except it's dark out. Come on."

Kit squared her shoulders and came but the journey was far from easy. The wind buffeted them every step of the way. The driving rain struck at their faces. Ellen dragged Rosemary along resolutely. Martha and Kit followed, Martha hauling Kit along too, not because of her fear but simply because she was so lightly built she would have made no headway on her own. They passed several cottages with lights but Ellen refused to stop.

"It isn't much further to Dr. Hill's," she shouted over the noise of the storm, "and we'll only have to explain once."

"I still feel fine," Rosemary shouted in return. "I have a stitch in my side. But I think it's from rushing!"

"People never do feel anything till just at the last," Martha yelled and wished she hadn't.

Rosemary staggered on without another word.

Then they were there. Dr. Hill's lights were on. Ellen hammered on the door. It seemed to take him forever to answer.

"What is it?" he asked, opening the door a crack and peering out at the dripping huddle of girls.

"Martha's poisoned Rosemary," Ellen told him, gasping for breath between the words.

She steadied herself, gulped in more air and went on quickly.

"Only it was hardly anything, just a blob, so I don't think she did, except it does say 'for external use only' so we couldn't sit and wait in case . . ."

Till that moment, though Martha had been worried, she had not had time to give in to the grip of real terror. Now faced by the solid reality of Dr. Hill, she began to shake. Her teeth clattered. Her hands curled up into knots.

Please, please, let it be all right, she begged inside her head. Please, don't let her die.

"Come on in and calm down," Dr. Hill said, opening his door wide. When they were inside, he took the tube of ointment which Ellen had brought along and read the label. He gave Rosemary one keen look. Then, incredibly, he began to laugh.

156

"Won't do you a bit of harm, young lady," he said, still chuckling. "Might even do you good if you've scraped your esophagus lately."

Martha stared at him as he went on making jokes. He was silly. He was heartless. She hated him.

But I'm not a murderer! she thought suddenly.

Then she was laughing too. The doctor was stupid, but she was so weak with relief she either had to laugh or cry.

"You'd better stay here till it calms down outside," Dr. Hill said then. "How's the arm, Martha?"

"It won't calm down for days probably," Martha burst out rudely, ignoring his query. She could not stand to stay there talking. She wanted to be back out in the Blow, cleansed by the cold rain, freed by the tumultuous wind, away from Dr. Hill's amused grin, far away from her own terror which now seemed ridiculous. Without a word of farewell, she yanked the door open and plunged through. Kit followed on her heels. Ellen and Rosemary stopped to say thank you and good-bye, but they did not dally over it. Then they were on their way home, the wind behind them at last.

" 'O Canada, my home and native land . . .' " Martha shouted into the wind, needing to let her feelings out in some grand way.

" 'Oh, say can you see by the dawn's early light,' " Kit came in unexpectedly, singing against her.

Hand in hand, the two of them ran and sang, both of them missing the tunes by miles. Then the others

157

joined in, each of them adding her voice to her younger sister's. They battled through to the end of the first verses of both national anthems. Then Kit said, "Teach us yours."

"What?" Martha bellowed.

"Teach us yours," Kit shouted back.

It meant singing at the tops of their voices, but by the time they were back at the Winstons' cottage, the American girls knew all the "We stand on guard" parts.

Ellen fetched towels. First they dried themselves as best they could. Then they mopped up the floor.

"Let's get into our pajamas," Martha suggested.

They ran upstairs and changed. When they were back in the living room with the fire going, Ellen said shyly, "Now we ought to learn *your* national anthem."

"I already know it," Martha claimed. She felt cocky and wonderful. "Last year in choir we learned a whole bunch of national anthems."

"Well, teach me then," Ellen said.

So Rosemary, Kit and Martha sang while Ellen hummed along.

"This is kind of like camp," Kit whispered to Martha in the middle of singing. "We sing there every night almost, around the campfire."

"It isn't really a campfire," Martha said. "But it's better than nothing," she added, smiling to herself.

"What's funny about that?" Kit asked.

"Nothing. I'm just happy, I guess." Martha

158

dodged the question. She had still not told Kit her dream of a camp at the cottage. "What other songs do you know?"

They all knew "I've Been Working on the Railroad" and "We Shall Overcome." They knew most of "Waltzing Matilda."

"How about 'Edelweiss'?" Ellen wanted to know.

"Hey! I know a better one for us. The perfect one," Martha cried.

"What?" Kit questioned, since Martha was waiting to be asked.

" 'Blowing in the Wind'!"

They laughed and sang it. Then Martha, running out of inspiration and energy at the same moment, said sleepily, "I wish Mother was here to read to us."

"Maybe we could read to each other instead," Rosemary said unexpectedly, sounding as shy as Kit.

"Yeah," Martha said eagerly, waking up. "Ellen, you pick. But not one of Arthur Ransome's."

"What's wrong with Arthur Ransome?" Kit asked, not shyly at all. "They're my favorite books."

Martha made a face.

"The kids work too hard," she said. "They're always putting up tents or scrubbing decks or going for milk."

"Nobody in an Arthur Ransome book ever reminded me of you, Martha," Ellen said as the rest laughed. "I know someone who does, though. Belinda in *Miss Happiness and Miss Flower*."

Martha stared at her older sister. She was not sure

whether to be pleased or not. She herself liked Belinda, but she recognized her faults. Belinda was rough and tough. She was brave too, but she could be mean. She played practical jokes. Martha felt her stomach tighten. Belinda had never murdered anybody.

But I didn't either, Martha reminded herself.

Then she realized what the others were saying. Neither of the Swann girls had read either *Miss Happiness and Miss Flower* or its sequel, *Little Plum.*

"Is she really like Martha? Let's read it," Kit urged.

"It's a bit young, really," Ellen hedged, looking at Rosemary.

"Do you still like it?" Rosemary asked.

Ellen nodded.

"Then I will too," Rosemary said comfortably. "I still love *Winnie-the-Pooh.*"

"Let's read in our beds," Martha said. "I mean Kit and me in our beds and you two come in there."

Ten minutes later they were set. Martha snuggled down under the covers. She felt good all over. Rosemary was fine and the supper had been a success . . .

"Ellen," she burst out. "We didn't have any supper!"

"Oh, for heaven's sake! I completely forgot," Ellen said. "But now you mention it, I'm starving."

160

"Allow me to butter you a pancake," Rosemary offered, and even Martha laughed shakily.

"I'll go down and make us some sandwiches," Ellen said.

"I'll help." Kit went too.

Soon everyone felt better. When the last crumb was demolished and the last drop of milk drained, Ellen held out the book to Rosemary.

"You start," she said.

Rosemary began—and they were in England with Nona, the other heroine. She was so lonely, so left out, a bit silly, but real.

And if I'm like Belinda, I know who used to be like Nona, Martha thought, glancing sideways at Kit.

Then she forgot both herself and Kit in the magic of the story.

14 | Rosemary Decides

The storm blew itself out during the night. In the morning, Martha knelt on her bed and looked out through the small window at the beach.

"It looks all . . . polished," she said, searching for a better word but not finding it.

Kit came and looked over her shoulder. It seemed a world made new. The water sparkled. The sky was definitely brighter and bluer. And the sun shed a different light.

"Yeah," Kit answered Martha's statement. "I know what you mean."

Then they heard Ellen moan.

It was a cry of such anguish that they sprang up and went clattering down the stairs. Ellen was standing staring into the kitchen.

"It is a shambles," she told them. "It is a disaster. It is a catastrophe. And it's going to take us the whole morning to clean it up."

"Not me," said Martha promptly. "I have a broken arm."

"Tough about your arm," Ellen said. "You can

put things away, if nothing else. You MADE lots of this mess, don't forget."

After breakfast, she got them organized. Rosemary washed piles of dishes. Kit dried; Martha put away. She had to put each plate, every glass in its place one at a time, but Ellen said that was fine, just so they got there. Ellen herself went about picking up, scraping, organizing, and generally finding more work for everybody else.

"I didn't know we HAD this many dishes," Martha complained after half an hour.

"Don't forget we got three suppers ready last night and didn't clean up after any of them," Ellen said.

Martha silently took the first of the large plates from Kit and reached to put it in its place. Something was wrong. The plate refused to sit properly on the shelf. Puzzled, Martha took it down, set it on the counter in a clear corner and examined the shelf. There was a pebble lying there. How it got there she could not figure out, but she recognized it. The wishing stone Bruce had found for her!

She took it in her hand and held it, enjoying its roundness and smooth surface. What had her wish been exactly? She knew it had had something to do with camp, but she could not remember how it had gone.

It sure didn't come true anyway, she thought, and moved to toss the pebble into the garbage.

No. Bruce had gone to too much trouble to find it. Maybe it only worked on Thursdays or when you rubbed it a certain way. She shoved it into her jeans pocket and put the plate in place. Then she picked up the frying pan. Holding it, she paused.

"What's come over you?" Ellen asked, bumping into her.

"I was thinking about everything that's happened," Martha said. "We just met a couple of days ago, and yet I feel as though we've been here for years."

"That dash to the doctor's!" Rosemary said, shuddering.

"Feeding the gulls," Kit said, taking the frying pan from Martha and putting it away herself as she spoke.

"Those terrible pork chops," Ellen remembered. "I don't think I ever want to eat pork chops again."

"What did you do to them anyway?" Martha wanted to know.

"Never you mind," Ellen told her.

"I learned to play gin rummy," Kit said.

There was a note of pride in her voice. No wonder, Martha thought.

"How about our bat hunt?" she herself exclaimed.

"I'd almost forgotten that," Rosemary said.

The younger girls laughed.

"You never knew the really exciting part," Martha said.

She told the dramatic tale of the midnight rescue.

"You goons! He might have bitten one of you," Ellen said. But she did not sound too upset. Like Rosemary's trip to the doctor, it was safely in the past.

Rosemary turned her back suddenly. She spoke over her shoulder.

"You know something I think you've all maybe forgotten?"

"What?" the other three chorused, ready to go on reliving their experiences.

"Today's Wednesday," Rosemary said.

"Is it?" Martha said after a second. "So what?"

Then she saw Kit's face and Ellen's and she remembered. On Wednesday, she was going to escape from being cooped up at the cottage with the Swann girls. On Wednesday their mothers were coming to take them back to town.

Martha felt shaken. She had not thought about Wednesday coming for ages. Now Rosemary had reminded her, and she knew, all at once, that she did not want to be rescued. She wanted to stay right here, to add to their growing list of adventures, to become closer to the others in a way she was certain they could never do in town, not with grown-ups watching and little brothers tagging after them.

But what about the rest? Nobody was saying a word.

Then Rosemary spoke again, breaking the silence

her first words had created. "Hey, we're finished. The kitchen's actually clean!"

"Thank goodness," said Martha automatically.

"You can say that again," cried Ellen. "Here come both of our mothers right this instant."

The other three girls ran to peer out the back window too. Yes, Nell Swann and Caroline Winston were on their way up the walk. Ellen whirled around and faced the others.

"Not a word about that bat," she warned.

"Or about the ointment," Martha cried.

"Nothing that would worry them," Ellen agreed, "no matter what."

Kit and Rosemary nodded.

"Anybody home?" Ellen's mother called through the screen door.

"Sure!" Ellen answered. Then, with great surprise in her voice, she exclaimed, "Why, Mother! . . . I mean, I never thought you'd be here so early. You must have got up at dawn."

"It's cooler driving then," her mother said, smiling at the spic-and-span kitchen. "How have you been getting along on your own? Any emergencies?"

"Nothing we couldn't handle."

"Everything was fine, Mrs. Winston."

"We were okay."

"Oh, Mother, of course not!"

"That's wonderful," Caroline Winston said, although Martha had a feeling she was wondering what had really happened. Mother was pretty smart.

Then Mrs. Swann turned to Kit and said in a low voice, "I thought of you, darling, during that dreadful, dreadful windstorm! Were you very frightened out here all by yourself?"

Martha winced. No wonder Kit was scared to death of storms.

But Rosemary was the one who answered.

"Kit was just fine, Mother," she said crisply. "And she wasn't by herself; she was right here with us."

She called her Kit, Martha thought, feeling dazed. Had Rosemary done it on purpose?

Kit, chin high, looked straight at her mother as though she planned to make a great announcement.

"I was okay," she said.

Though Martha could hardly hear her, she did know Kit had neither looked at her feet nor stammered.

"Well, I'm just so proud of you, baby," Mrs. Swann said. Turning to the rest of them, she added, "Everybody all packed and ready for the trip back to civilization?"

"Well, not exactly," Ellen said. "To tell you the truth, I'd forgotten what day it was."

"Me too," Martha said, looking straight at her mother.

Kit nodded her head.

"I guess I'm the only one who remembered," Rosemary said. "I'm ready whenever everybody else is."

"You others had better get a move on," Mrs.

Swann said brightly. "I might have known, Rosemary, that you'd be the one counting the days."

"I wasn't," Rosemary said. "I just remembered, that's all."

Caroline Winston looked at the other three girls. Not one had started for the stairs. They were just standing there, not moving, stealing sidelong looks at each other.

"Well, what about it?" she asked, giving them their chance. "I have a feeling that the decision to go back to town isn't exactly unanimous."

"I want to stay here," Martha said.

"I don't want to go either," Ellen backed her up. "It's so hot in town and crowded. But if Rosemary . . ."

Her voice trailed off.

"I'm packed," Rosemary said. "I thought we were all going. We can do things there, different kinds of things. . . ."

Then Kit amazed them by deciding for everyone.

"I want to stay here too," she said, looking at Martha's mother rather than her own. "If Rosemary wants to go, it would still be okay if the rest of us stayed, wouldn't it?"

"I don't see why not," Caroline Winston said. "Let's get your things out to the car, Rosemary."

She went out to the car. Rosemary disappeared up the stairs to fetch her suitcase. When she came down, she had her head high but she paused and looked at the others.

"I thought everyone would come," Rosemary said. "We agreed on Sunday that we'd all go today."

"We changed our minds," Martha told her.

Mrs. Swann called. Rosemary hesitated a moment longer. Then she went out to the car. The younger girls went to the back door to see her leave. Ellen joined them.

Rosemary waved. They waved back. The car was gone.

The three who were left turned back into the cottage. It felt empty.

"She didn't want to go either," Martha said.

"That's what I think too," Ellen said, "but why didn't she say so? The rest of us did."

"Rosemary has trouble backing down," Kit said. There was no blame in her words, only helplessness.

"What'll we do now?" Martha asked as cheerfully as she could.

"Go swimming, I guess," Ellen said. "It feels so queer doing things without her. But I guess we might as well go swimming."

It felt queer without Rosemary all day long.

15 | New Arrivals

Martha was dropping off to sleep that night when Kit spoke.

"If we'd asked her to stay, she would have," Kit said.

"We were really dumb," Martha said, not needing to ask whom she meant. "Maybe we can phone in the morning."

"That might work," Kit said slowly. "We could try. Remember how I told you Mother says Rosemary's her girl and I'm Dad's? And I said we were different from you and Ellen . . . ?"

"Yeah," Martha said as Kit hesitated, groping for words.

"Well, I thought that was true. I thought she was mean and I didn't care about her. And then, the other night, when Ellen said you'd maybe poisoned her . . ."

"That was just last night," Martha said, marveling.

"Last night then, when I thought she might— something might happen to her, I found out I care about her a lot more than I knew."

"She's your sister," Martha said. "There's no getting around it; sisters matter."

"When I was little, she used to pull me on a sled all the way to the library and she made up a game about us being Eskimos," Kit said.

"Rosemary?" Martha found this hard to imagine.

"She's a lot nicer than you think," Kit said, on the defensive. "Last year I wanted a dog for my birthday and she went to the SPCA and brought home a puppy."

"I didn't know you had a dog." Martha was wide-awake now, fascinated by the new picture Kit was painting of her sister.

"I don't. Mother didn't want him and Mrs. Neville turned out to be allergic to dog hair," Kit said. "But Rosemary cried as much as I did when we had to take him back. You know, I was thinking that Ellen ought to do the phoning—but maybe I could."

"We'll all talk," Martha decided, "but you should go first."

"Or maybe Ellen first," Kit said, weakening. "Then I could just say 'Me too.' "

In the morning, though, Kit did make the phone call. They all waited, holding their breaths, while the rings sounded. Six. Seven. Eight . . .

"Everybody's out," Kit said. "Even Rosemary!"

"They can't be." Ellen took the receiver out of her hand. "You must have made a mistake when you dialed. It's not even nine o'clock."

171

But still the phone went unanswered.

"That's crazy," Ellen said, hanging up. "Maybe something's still wrong because of the lines being down the other day—although it sounded perfectly normal. I want to wash my hair before I get dressed. As soon as I'm finished, we'll try again."

She went upstairs. Kit turned to Martha.

"They might have slept right through it," she said. "Or just didn't want to answer."

"Not Toby," Martha said. "Answering the telephone is one of his favorite things and he wakes up at dawn."

She remembered her telephone conversation with Toby a few days before. She was thankful now that she had failed to reach her mother that morning.

"I don't know if I can do it next time," Kit said, her eyes meeting Martha's. "While I was waiting, I couldn't think of how to begin."

"Don't panic," Martha said. "She's only your sister, not some monster. The very worst thing she can say is she wouldn't come back out here for all the tea in China."

"I know," said Kit. "That's what I'm scared of."

Then Martha thought of Rosemary the way she had been the night the Swanns arrived. Suppose that was the girl they got on the phone and she asked in her coldest voice, "Why on earth would I want to come back to that cabin?" Martha tried to think of what she would answer. She found not one single

172

helpful word inside her head. Glad that the asking was not going to be up to her, she gave Kit a comforting pat on the shoulder.

"You'll do fine," she said.

An hour later, after they had tried three more times, they were forced to give up.

"There's nothing else we can do except call the neighbors," Ellen said, "and I'd feel silly trying to explain. I mean, why shouldn't they go out if they want to? They're probably in some obvious place we just haven't thought of. In the meantime, we might as well go swimming."

"That's exactly what you said yesterday after Rosemary left—'We might as well go swimming,'" Martha remembered. She shrugged off the uneasiness they were all feeling. "Come on then. Let's get moving. The water looks really warm."

"You can't tell temperature by looking—" Ellen began.

A car pulled up behind the cottage and the horn sounded—a long, a short, and a long.

"Dad!" Martha cried, and ran.

As she came flying out of the cottage, Mr. Winston opened the car door. Bruce jumped out first. Toby, pushing, was right behind him. Then, only a little more slowly, Rosemary emerged, tugging her suitcase after her.

"Good morning, Martha," her father said. "We're planning to start charging for taxi service. But right now, lend a hand. I have to be back in town half an hour ago."

Martha, laughing at him, started to obey and almost banged into Rosemary.

"Am I ever glad to see you!" she burst out, not even thinking of looking for the right words.

"Am I ever glad to be back!" Rosemary responded with a funny little grin. "However, it's a long story and your Dad's in a big hurry. Hi, Christine. Help bring in the company's sleeping bags."

"Sleeping bags!" Martha yelped.

"That's what I said," Rosemary replied. And the next thing Martha knew, Rosemary had dumped her suitcase onto the ground and she and Ellen were hugging each other like long-lost friends.

That *is* sort of how it feels, Martha thought, while Kit tucked a neatly rolled sleeping bag under her good arm for her. Even if she has only been gone one day.

In fifteen minutes, the car was unloaded and Mr. Winston, wishing them luck as he left, drove off.

Ellen, Martha and Kit had been kept too busy to find out what had made Rosemary come back and why she had brought the boys along. Toby and Bruce, capering with excitement, had strangely little to say.

"I'll explain everything," Rosemary announced, "only let's go inside and sit down first. Okay. Now we're settled. Remember what you promised, boys!"

Toby nodded. Bruce looked a little embarrassed.

"She bribed us not to talk," he told Ellen. "With Popsicles."

"Were they good?" Ellen asked, smiling at him.

"Yup. Mine was blueberry." He stuck out a blue tongue to prove it.

"Bruce, sit down and be quiet," Rosemary said.

"Order in the court. The monkey wants to speak," Ellen teased.

Rosemary laughed with the rest of them. Then she launched into her story.

"First of all, you three were horrible yesterday just standing there and saying good-bye to me as if I didn't belong. I know, I know! I said I wanted to go and I thought I meant it. But I never dreamed you weren't going to come too. And I didn't know how to back down when they were waiting for me and not one of you said 'Stay'!"

"Kit was right," Martha interrupted. "She said you had trouble backing down and you'd have stayed if we'd asked you."

Rosemary looked over at Kit, curled up in a corner of the chesterfield.

"If you were so smart, Christine, why didn't you speak up?" she demanded.

Kit cleared her throat, stared at Toby's cowlick and muttered, "I didn't . . . You wouldn't . . . I thought maybe I was wrong."

"And you didn't think I'd listen anyway," Rosemary said for her. "Probably I wouldn't have. But you cannot imagine how gruesome it was being in town last night. Mother and I went to a movie and I couldn't keep my mind on it because I kept wondering what you guys were doing. Then, afterward, Mother made this big speech about how sorry she was I hadn't had a chance to go to Nancy Elliot's. I didn't know what to say back, because the whole idea of going there seems so unreal now. Nancy's okay but there's so little to do there."

Martha stared at her. She had thought going to visit Nancy meant as much to Rosemary as going to camp meant to her. It had helped her forgive some of Rosemary's nagging at Kit, knowing how disappointed she felt inside about what she was missing.

I still wish I'd gone to camp, don't I? Martha asked herself.

And in spite of all that was happening at the cottage, she knew she did. Of course, if she had, she would never have known Kit.

"They found a bat once when I was at Nancy's," Rosemary said, recapturing Martha's attention. "That's where I heard about the broom. But do you know what we actually did? We all went into the living room and closed the doors and waited until their handyman came and told Mrs. Elliot they had caught it and we could come out. Everybody talked and talked about it but nobody ever once saw it except for Nancy's aunt and the servants. Everything there is like that. Meals just happen. They beat on a gong and you go. And there aren't any books. Just magazines. Not that that has anything to do with what I'm telling you."

Martha had to make sure. She interrupted again. "You mean you're glad you didn't get to go there? You'd rather be here?"

Rosemary shifted on her chair, gave her long hair the familiar toss back and looked as though she wished Martha would stick to listening.

"I didn't say that exactly," she said. "And, Christine, you don't need to go running to Dad and tell him I said any such thing. He'd say 'I told you so!' and there's nothing wrong with Nancy. Not a thing!"

"Can we talk now?" asked Toby, as she stopped to draw a deep breath.

"No!" Rosemary exploded. Then she burst out laughing at the mixture of expressions on the faces around her and, even more, at herself.

"I'd much rather be here," she said. "And that is exactly what your mother figured out. She knocked on my door last night and when she came in, she said, 'You want to go back to the cottage, don't you, Rosemary?' I didn't have to think twice. I practically yelled 'Yes!' at her. 'Well, the boys have been tormenting me to let them spend a day there,' she said, 'so you might as well all go together in the morning.' She went and told my mother, who is still in a state of shock. Then she asked your father to take us and come back tonight for the boys because they, the mothers that is, had arranged to go to the Stratford Festival for the day and they wouldn't be back till after midnight. Mr. Winston said he could deliver us if we started really early but he couldn't come and get Toby and Bruce because he'd set up an interview in the evening and so—"

"WE GET TO STAY ALL NIGHT!" Toby shouted, unable to keep still one moment longer.

Bruce, eyes shining, stood up and came over to Martha.

"Now we can be in it too, can't we, Marth?" he said. "We didn't ask her anything about it last night because there was always somebody listening and we could tell it was a secret."

"I almost said something," Toby confessed, "but Bruce stopped me in time. He figured out it must be a secret because Rosemary never said a word about it no matter what the grown-ups asked her."

Martha was mystified.

"Be in what?" she asked.

Then, in a flash, she remembered the nonsense she had told Bruce that long-ago morning on the swings. She jumped up.

"Never mind." She tried to stop them explaining. Bruce sensed her dismay and waited.

But Toby felt no uncertainty.

"We can be part of the camp, Martha," he said.

He bounced up and down, his joy acting like a pogo stick.

178

"The camp, the camp, the camp!" he sang. "We can be part of the camp."

He hushed. The other three girls turned, as one, and looked at Martha.

"What camp?" they asked.

16 | Orienteering

Martha wished they would stop staring at her that way. She could feel them waiting for her answer and she did not want to explain. But she did not want Bruce to explain either and she knew that if she didn't, he would.

"Well, you see . . . um . . . I told Bruce . . ." she began.

She was getting nowhere fast when she saw understanding dawn on Ellen's face. Martha did not know whether to be glad or sorry. What had Bruce told them when he ran home that day? Ellen walked over to Bruce and put her arm around his shoulders.

"Martha was just kidding," she said. "I'm sorry if you counted on it, but we couldn't really have a camp, not with only four of us."

"You don't have a camp?"

Ellen shook her head. Bruce stared up at her, still hoping she was mistaken.

"You don't blow a whistle to get them up?" he asked, his hope wavering.

"No whistle," Ellen said. She gave Martha a dirty look over the top of his head. Martha knew she deserved it. If only Bruce hadn't believed her!

"But there IS a whistle," Toby put in.

Ellen looked at him in surprise. Sometimes their mother did use a whistle to summon them in out of the water.

"I guess Mother's whistle is upstairs somewhere, if that's what you mean," she said.

"Then we could start the camp today," Toby said. He checked them all, making sure he was right before he added, "There's six people here, not four. Six would be enough."

"Would somebody mind explaining what you are all talking about?" Rosemary asked.

"Go right ahead, Martha," Ellen said.

Martha had to go back to the beginning. As she struggled through her story, the others saw plainly how miserable she had felt that morning, faced with the fact that Tracey was going to camp while she had to stay behind. Also, without intending to, she let slip how she and Ellen had dreaded being hauled back to town to entertain visitors they did not even know. Before she finished, her face grew very red and her voice wobbled.

Rosemary straightened in her chair and immediately caught hold of the conversation.

"I don't see why we can't play we're camping just for today. We have to baby-sit anyway."

Toby scowled at her and Bruce said, "I am seven going on eight."

"No offense meant," Rosemary said, laughing.

That's her poised laugh, Martha thought. She thinks they're funny. But she likes them.

"I always enjoyed camp when I went," Rosemary went on. "We used to have a great time. Geraldine and Diane and I stayed awake for hours talking. One year Diane brought fifty-three *Love Comics* with her!"

Martha was floored by this last speech. First she had never dreamed that Rosemary would have liked camp. And, second, camp the way Rosemary described it was nothing like the camp Martha so longed to attend. *Love Comics!*

Bruce, who delighted in comics, beamed at Rosemary. Toby began to caper with excitement. Ellen grew quickly practical.

"Okay. Suppose we do play this is a camp. Don't get your hopes up yet, boys. What would we DO? Besides blowing the whistle."

She was looking right at Rosemary. With a dry note in her voice that made Martha want to cheer, she inquired, "What did *you* do—other than read *Love Comics*?"

"We square danced," Rosemary said. "But we don't have the right music here and I've forgotten how mostly."

"Dancing!" Toby sounded horrified.

182

"We learned to canoe and ride horseback." Rosemary forged on quickly, not needing to be told these were not helpful suggestions. "We played games. Baseball and stuff."

"We play games every day at the park," Bruce said. "Besides, we're no good at baseball, are we, Toby?"

Toby took a mighty swing with an imaginary bat to demonstrate how wrong Bruce was. Then he said, "Nuts on baseball."

"Discussion groups? Weaving?" Rosemary was running out. She brightened. "They taught me to swim."

"We can swim already," Toby informed her.

Martha knew he always kept one foot touching bottom but she did not tell.

They were getting nowhere and even Bruce began to look discouraged. Yet if only somebody would come up with the right idea, Martha could tell that both Rosemary and Ellen would go along with it. To them, it was a game, a way to keep the boys amused, but it meant much more than that to her.

And it just might work, she thought. It might turn out to be real.

"Kit," she said, "how about your camp?"

"We go on hikes and swim and ride and go canoeing too," Kit said slowly. "But there are other special groups you go in depending on your interests. Leather Work. Star Study."

183

"It's daytime," Bruce mentioned.

"Or you can join Orienteering or . . ." Kit floundered.

"What's that? Ori— what you said?" Toby pounced on the new word.

Kit looked vague.

"I've never done it," she said. "I was in Drama and Sketching. But kids I know tried it. You go out in the bush and then you make a map of what you find and blaze trails and look for moss. You find your way back by the sun. It's in case you get lost in the wilderness," she finished.

"Lost in the wilderness!" Bruce crooned the words.

Toby went charging around the room, coming to an abrupt stop in front of Martha.

"Don't just sit there, Marth," he ordered. "We gotta get ready. We're a camp and we're going Ori . . ."

"Orienteering," Bruce helped him out.

"But nobody has a clue how to do it!" Rosemary was unable to believe her ears. "Sketching, now—we COULD do that."

The boys ignored her.

"Do you have to be lost by yourself?" Bruce asked Kit, his eyes anxious.

"I think you do it in teams. You take a knife and maybe matches."

"Ellen, Kit and me are one team," Toby decided.

184

"You three can be the other. What else do you take, Kit?"

She just stared at him blankly.

"Canteens," Bruce said. "And a compass. Only we don't have one that works."

"Too bad," Toby said. His brow furrowed in thought and then cleared. "We ought to take a lunch. Shouldn't we, Martha?"

"I think you're supposed to gnaw on edible roots," Kit said, laughter in her voice although her face stayed poker straight.

Martha jumped to her feet.

"We can take thermoses for canteens. Definitely we take a lunch. We'll pretend it's roots. . . . We *are* going, aren't we?"

"Trust Christine to come up with a bright idea like this!" Rosemary said. Then she relented and grinned at Martha, making Martha remember how they had missed her the day before. "Sure. Let's go. What have we got to lose?"

"Okay, Toby," Ellen said as they left the house later. "Lead the way."

Toby looked up and down the beach.

"Where's the best wilderness?" he asked.

"Not the pines. We can't get lost there," Bruce said.

He was right. The small stand of pines directly across the back lane from the cottage was a favorite play place. Every tree, almost every root, was famil-

185

iar. Suddenly Martha felt despairing. There were no real woods nearby, just sand dunes and brush. The river, she knew from past experience, was too far. And it was not mysterious either. Their Orienteering was over before it began.

The boys were not so easily defeated.

"You have to explore," Toby said. "I'll start my tribe along the beach and you go that way."

Obediently Martha and Rosemary set off after Bruce. They trudged along for what seemed like hours. The sun grew hotter and hotter. Whenever Bruce led the way through grass, swarms of angry mosquitoes rose to attack them. There was also a bee.

It doesn't even know I'm here, Martha tried to convince herself.

The bee roared by within an inch of her left ear. Martha marched on, her gaze set.

"Rosemary, make this bee go away from me," she said out of the corner of her mouth.

"Bee!" Rosemary cried and backed speedily away from her teammate. "Just keep moving. If you don't agitate him, you'll be fine."

"He's agitating ME!" Martha said through stiff lips.

"Don't be scared of a bee, Martha," Bruce said from somewhere near her elbow. "Bees are interesting."

Martha, with the bee hovering and buzzing right over her head, remembered herself telling Kit that storms were really fun. Faced by the reality of one large rumbling bumblebee, Martha felt ashamed of herself. Who was she to call anyone else a mouse!

"There it goes," Bruce said. "It's looking for honey."

Martha sighed with relief and swatted a mosquito.

"Martha," Bruce said, "when do we start being lost?"

"Oh, Bruce, it's only a game," Rosemary said, sounding as if she knew exactly how he felt all the same. "There isn't any real wilderness."

Martha knew she was right. All they could really do was go on a hike, have a picnic and come home. Right from where they stood, she could see four cottages and she recognized them all. Even if they went for miles, there would be no wilderness, only scrubby brush like the stuff by the river.

Maybe if they cut up to the golf course they would find some real trees. It would be a tame woods and there were always golfers looking for lost balls but it might be better than nothing. She remembered that that had been her name for this make-believe camp but she was too dispirited to smile.

"Oh, Martha," Bruce cried out, startling her, "I fear I cannot go one step farther."

The next instant, he sprawled on the sand at her feet. Martha was frightened till she saw his brown eyes gleaming up at her. "Give me water," he gasped. "Water! I beg of you!"

Martha pulled back her foot to give him a good

kick instead. He was spoiling everything. Then Rosemary astonished both of them by dropping to her knees beside him. She unscrewed the top of the thermos, poured a little water into the lid, and, supporting Bruce with her other arm, held it to his lips.

"Drink, brave lad," she told him. "Thou has earned it this day."

"Hey, quit that. . . ." Martha started, her voice rising in protest. "We're Orienteering."

Bruce let his eyelids flutter. He raised one weak hand to steady the cup, took a small sip and let his head fall back on Rosemary's shoulder.

"I am a trifle weak from loss of blood," he whispered, "but I can still fight on for the Cause."

Rosemary forgot her part momentarily and snickered.

"What Cause?" Martha demanded, glaring. "What loss of blood?"

Bruce stopped acting and looked up at her.

"Aw Martha," he said, "it's no fun just walking and walking."

Martha could not ague with that. But what about her dream of a camp? Then, glancing from his face to Rosemary's, she faced the fact that even if she did make him give up pretending, their plan to try Orienteering was not going to work.

But I play like this every time I baby-sit, she thought.

Not with Rosemary and Kit though, another voice inside her said.

"Thou art a brave fellow, knave," she said, giving in. "Didst thou sight the enemy along the way?"

Beaming, Bruce sprang to his feet, his loss of blood no longer troubling him.

"That I did," he cried. Pointing with a flourish, he indicated Toby's team toiling along the beach about a hundred yards away. "Yonder rides the wicked Sheriff of Nottingham with his surly henchmen. Let us prepare an ambush."

"Too late," Martha said. "The villain hast spotted you."

Bruce, giving a battle cry that sounded more like Tarzan than Robin Hood, took off, his two merry men scrambling to keep up with him.

From then on, they were all engaged in a great and glorious battle. Roughly halfway through, everyone had to change identity and Martha learned that she was the Sheriff's two-hundred-year-old mother, trying to sneak away with the money bags hidden under her cloak. Both Robins triumphed and both Sheriffs were left penniless, gnashing their teeth and swearing vengeance.

"Hey, I'm starving," Toby said, mopping his face with his shirt.

Martha sank down thankfully and undid the sandwiches, which she had kept safe throughout all the excitement.

"Have some venison," she invited, "and open that flagon of whatever it is."

"Lemonade," Bruce said.

"It ought to be ale," Rosemary said.

"Lemonale then," Bruce corrected himself.

They ate in contented silence. Then Bruce, pointing at Martha, said, "We would have won both times if Little John hadn't been wounded."

"Let's start again as soon as we've finished eating," Toby said, talking with his mouth full.

Ellen spoke with extreme firmness. She sounded exactly like Mother. "We are going home and cleaning up and then you are going in swimming."

Toby looked around at them all. "At camp, everyone has to go in together, don't they?" he said.

"Of course," Bruce answered.

Martha tried again to believe this was like camp. After all they were eating outside. Kids at camp did that all the time. But they were not eating camp food. They had just polished off a chocolate cake Mother had sent along with the boys. And Martha had never heard of a camp where you played Robin Hood.

Suddenly Toby leaped up, ran at her and gave her a strangling hug. "I'm so glad we have a camp, Marth!" he cried.

Martha gasped, straightened her sling as he let go of her and smiled at him.

"Forsooth, varlet, I am right glad to hear it," she said.

And she was.

The afternoon was almost as hectic as the morning.

190

"Don't they ever run down?" Rosemary asked.

But nighttime finally came. Ellen talked of building a campfire but by five the sky had clouded over and it was growing cold. They built a fire in the fireplace instead and toasted marshmallows. They sang too.

It should be like a real camp, Martha thought.

Yet the songs they were singing were those the small boys knew. And Martha was kept busy helping them hold their marshmallows at the right angle. She could not be a camper and a big sister at the same time.

"No, Toby! Don't swing it around!" she said as his marshmallow burst into flame. "Blow on it."

Kit set hers on fire the next minute.

"No, Christine. Don't wave it about," Rosemary mimicked Martha. "Blow on it!"

Kit had blown it out already but suddenly she looked younger, as though she really belonged with the little boys.

I missed Rosemary when she was gone, Martha thought, but she's still her charming old self, all right. Only why does Kit let herself be turned into a baby like that? They make me so tired!

"Who *are* you?" Toby asked Kit. At her look of confusion, he made his question clear. "I mean, are you really Christine or Kit? My long name's Tobias but I'm really Toby. And I don't like being called Tobias!" he added, giving Bruce a menacing look.

Kit put down her marshmallow stick and braced

herself with both hands on the floor behind her before she answered.

"My mother calls me Christine and that's my long name, the same as yours is Tobias," she said. "I don't mind my mother saying it but Dad calls me Kit. And Kit's who I really am."

"Okay, Kit," Toby said. "Ellen, I need another marshmallow."

"Well, well, little sister," Rosemary said, her voice cool. "You never told me that before."

Kit rounded on her. The flickering shadows hid her expression but her voice was strong and direct.

"You never asked me. Toby did," Kit said.

Martha wanted to cheer but she popped an untoasted marshmallow into her mouth and held her peace.

Rosemary was quiet for a while. Bruce told everyone about the paper-bag puppet he had made at the park. When Toby asked for his sixth marshmallow, Ellen shook her head and moved them well out of his reach.

"You'll be sick, you little pig," she said.

"I've only had one." Rosemary spoke from the chesterfield where she sat watching. "Would you toast one for me . . . Kit?"

"Sure." Kit thrust one onto the point of her stick. Then she hesitated. "I burn them sometimes," she said.

"I like them burnt as long as they aren't solid

charcoal," Rosemary said. "I feel worn out after this day we've been through. Maybe I'm getting old."

"I thought it was a great day," Toby said. "I'm not a bit tired and I'm five."

As they laughed at him, Kit began toasting Rosemary's marshmallow. She turned it slowly, kept it close to a glowing coal but away from the flames, till it was a perfect golden brown all over. Martha watched with admiration. She always got impatient and let hers catch fire, trying to hurry them.

Kit rose, finally, and took the marshmallow, still on the stick, over to her sister.

"Be careful," she warned. "It's really hot."

"It is beautiful," Rosemary said. "Thanks, Kit. I'll appoint you my personal Marshmallow Toaster."

Martha, listening, thought it sounded too good to be true. Never mind. It was great while it lasted.

Ellen looked at the clock, got up and unrolled the boys' sleeping bags.

"Bedtime," she said.

Protesting all the way, the boys got into their pajamas, brushed their teeth and were tucked in.

Rosemary and Kit relaxed. Martha and Ellen, knowing their brothers, waited.

Martha saw Ellen silently slide her hand down beside the cushion on the chair where she sat. Her eyes, however, remained fixed on Toby.

"Ellen," Toby started, as his sisters had known he would.

Ellen's hand moved so quickly that Martha did not know what was coming. Then Ellen blew a piercing blast on the whistle. Toby, mouth ajar, stared at her.

"That," Ellen announced, "was the Lights-Out Whistle in this camp. All campers must now go right to sleep without one more word."

"You aren't even in bed," Bruce pointed out, "and you're campers too."

"Let's go right this minute," Rosemary said to Ellen. "A day of play with the children has worn me out."

Faker, Martha thought. You liked it.

"Okay," Ellen answered. "Camp . . ." She turned to Martha. "What's the name of this camp?" she asked.

The answer slipped out before Martha considered how it might sound. "Camp Better-Than-Nothing."

Kit giggled. Rosemary, in the middle of a yawn, stopped to chuckle.

"Camp Better-Than-Nothing now closes for the night," Ellen announced.

Half an hour later, the cottage was in darkness.

17 | Tin-Foil Dinners

"What are you doing with that?" Martha demanded as Ellen, Martha's rolled-up sleeping bag in her arms, came down the stairs.

"Mother's taking it back to town," Ellen said. "Well, you won't be using it, and I can hardly get around your junk in our room, so why not?"

"No reason," Martha said, and backed out of her way.

Ellen paused, hefted the sleeping bag so she could get a better grip and tried to make Martha smile.

"You still have your plastic soap dish, after all," she said, "and your flashlight with its brand-new batteries."

"Sure," Martha said.

She brushed past Ellen and ran upstairs as though she were in a hurry to get somewhere. Reaching the top, she stopped, at a loss what to do next. Then she went into the bathroom, shut the door, waited a moment, flushed the toilet, ran water into the basin, and emerged.

"Martha!" her mother called from the sun porch.

Martha ran back down, hoping her mother would not look at her too closely.

But Mother was rummaging in her purse. She was rushing because Toby and Bruce were already out in the car waiting for her, and Toby loved blowing the horn.

"Here," she said suddenly, handing Martha a postcard. "This came yesterday. Now I must be off. Are you sure you're all right?"

"We're fine." Ellen and Martha spoke together, and both Swann girls nodded their agreement. The horn gave its first long toot.

"Call if you need anything," Mother said.

When she was gone, Martha looked at her card. It had a picture of boys and girls swimming on the back, and on the front it read,

Dear Martha,
Wish you were here. It's great. Passed my
swimming test. Tin-foil dinner cookout to-
night. See you Sunday.

Love, Tracey.

"What is it, Martha?" Kit asked.

Wordlessly Martha handed over the card. Kit read it at a glance, returned it and said, "Well, at least she hasn't been Orienteering."

Martha thought of Tracey coming home with so much to tell about.

"Neither have we really," she said, not smiling.

Kit shrugged. "Tin-foil dinners aren't all that great. I've been on them. You aren't missing such a big deal."

"You have?" Martha said, her eyes widening.

"Sure," Kit said. "But all you do is cook a . . ."

The whole day changed for Martha. "We'll do it!" she cried. "If you know how . . ."

"Of course I know how," Kit said, "but I keep telling you . . ."

"Christine probably knows as much about tin-foil dinners as she did about Orienteering," Rosemary put in. "The great expert!"

Rosemary once more was back to being her old self. Kit too. She just stood there, not saying a word in her own defense.

Martha, her eyes angry, faced up to the older girl.

"Don't be so mean! If Kit says she knows how, she does. And it would be a real camp thing we could do. Not just playing with little kids like yesterday. I really, really want to do a true camp thing."

Ellen tried to calm them.

"Now, Martha, watch your temper," she said. "We're tired today. It would be awfully easy to get mad at each other for no good reason. Why don't we just take it easy? Read and swim and play games maybe and . . . People do those things at camp," she finished lamely.

Martha stared at her in horror.

"It's Friday," she pointed out as though Ellen had somehow lost track of time. "Kit and Rosemary are leaving on Sunday. We only have today and tomorrow left. We can play games and read when it rains or at night. But now is our chance."

Ellen sighed.

"But I've never made one of those tin-foil dinners," she began.

"Neither have I," Rosemary said, "and I hate cooking out anyway. Ashes get into things and bugs bite you."

Martha ignored Rosemary.

"Kit knows how exactly," she insisted. "And the tin foil keeps the ashes out, doesn't it, Kit?"

"Well, yeah, I guess so," Kit said. "But, Martha . . ."

"See. She doesn't know how any more than I do," Rosemary jeered.

"I've done it lots of times," Kit said with dignity. She hesitated, looking uneasy, and added, "The counselors helped, but I'm sure I remember."

"What do you have to have?" Ellen wanted to know. That might settle the whole question without any more argument.

"Carrots, onions, potatoes, hamburger," Kit listed off.

"We haven't any hamburger, and I'm pretty sure we're out of carrots," Ellen told Martha.

Martha took command. "We'll go and buy the stuff while you guys rest up and read or whatever dumb thing you want to do," she said. "Then this afternoon, you'll maybe be strong enough to come and help. You can put on bug spray," she added, finally looking at Rosemary.

"Okay, okay," Rosemary said. "But it had better be good."

Martha looked at Kit. Kit didn't say a word.

"It will be," Martha promised.

"And no tricks this time," Ellen warned.

"Of course not," Martha said. "Come on, Kit. Give us the money, Ellen. And we'll leave you two senior citizens in peace."

She laughed loudly at her own wit. Nobody joined in. Kit did not speak again until they were out of the house and on their way.

"I really DO know how to do them," she said then, "but lots of times, even when there's a counselor there, things go wrong."

"Not today they won't," Martha told her. "Today's my lucky day. And on Sunday I can tell Tracey."

Kit looked sideways at her.

"That's why you really want to do it, isn't it?" she asked.

"Not just," Martha said. She did not want to try

to explain. She had a feeling it would not make much sense. But Kit was still waiting.

"What, then?" she prompted.

"I just really want to camp," Martha confessed. "I know you don't like camping, but I'm positive I would. And I've been waiting so long. It seems long to me anyway."

"What do you expect camp to be like?" Kit was curious.

Martha was stumped. Her imagination presented her with a dozen pictures. Herself learning to dive properly. Stars shining through pine branches. Eating in a big dining hall and singing together—loud songs, crazy songs, the kind Martha loved. Talking in the cabin. Maybe telling ghost stories. Sitting on the hill where the chapel was and watching the sun set. Fishing. Learning how to do special outdoor things—like cooking tin-foil dinners.

"It isn't just the things you do at camp," she stumbled. "But every day is a special day somehow, isn't it?"

Kit thought back.

"Maybe," she said. "For you, it would be like that anyway."

"Hamburger and carrots—and anything else?" Martha asked.

"Maybe we ought to get an extra roll of tin foil in case we run out," Kit decided.

When they got home, Martha turned to Kit for directions.

"Just wait, Marth," Kit laughed. "We haven't even had lunch yet. You wanted to do this for supper, didn't you?"

Martha groaned, but managed to eat a good lunch in spite of her impatience to get started. After the dishes were out of the way, Kit challenged her to a few more hands of gin rummy. Since Kit was directing the tin-foil dinner making, Martha agreed—and was beaten again five games to three.

"Next time we're playing Monopoly," Martha stated, "or I'm not playing at all. I'm jinxed."

Then they swam.

"Now?" Martha demanded when they came up out of the water. "Can we start now?"

Kit looked up at the sun.

"I guess so," she said. "It takes a long time to get coals in the pit."

Coals! The pit! Martha shivered with pleasure.

"Ellen! Rosemary!" she yelled at the others, who were settling down to sunbathe. "Come ON! We're going to begin."

"Call us when you're finished and ready to serve us," Rosemary suggested, not moving.

But Ellen got to her feet and prodded Rosemary with her toe.

"Come on," she said. "We said we'd help."

201

Chadron State College Library
Chadron, Nebraska

"I did not," Rosemary declared.

"Sure you did," Ellen said, and hoisted her up. "Just think of how much you missed us all in town. Now we want you with us every minute."

"I should have listened to Mother," Rosemary lamented. "Oh for the bright lights and dens of iniquity."

The older girls were set to work chopping up the vegetables and making the meat into flat patties. Kit demonstrated, using a board covered with foil to do the slicing on.

"Just put everything in piles," she said, "while we get the fire started, and then I'll help you make them into packages."

"Packages!" Rosemary exclaimed, but Martha thought she looked at Kit with new respect. Martha herself was pleased with her friend. Kit sounded so sure, almost bossy.

"Now for the pit," she said, and she and Martha, using shovels belonging to Bruce and Toby, hollowed out a hole in the sand. The sides did not stay up exactly the way Kit thought they should.

"But it ought to do," she said, surveying it doubtfully.

"Blast!" Rosemary said, dropping a whole carrot into the sand. "And I'd just got it scraped."

"Never mind," Ellen said. "It's nice being this close to the house. Just go in and rinse it off."

"We need lots of wood," Kit was telling Martha, "and a hatchet to make the big chunks the right size."

Martha looked at her in dismay.

"We don't have a hatchet," she said. "Dad has one, but he never leaves it here because of Bruce and Toby."

Kit looked worried.

"Well, let's see what we can find," she said.

They hunted, but in the dunes near the cottage where they were having their cookout, there was little or nothing in the way of sticks. They did find some small stuff, and Martha proudly dragged back a huge pine branch which had blown down in the storm.

"Too green," Kit said, "and too big without a hatchet."

"I don't think it's too green," Martha said. It had been hard work bringing it all the way to the pit. "We can just stick one end in the fire when we get it going and push it in as it burns down."

"But it won't burn down," Kit said, her voice strained. "It's not dry."

Martha scowled. She still thought it looked pretty good. But she herself had made Kit the one in charge.

She sat back on her heels and watched Kit begin to build a fire with what sticks they had. When it

203

was ready to light, there were very few sticks left over. It did look like a real campfire though.

"Can I light it?" Martha begged.

"We're ready with the food," Ellen announced.

"Oh, dear!" Kit said. "Well, light the fire first, Marth. Here."

She handed Martha a book of matches. Martha fumbled with it. Kit reached out and took it back.

"You can't do it with one hand," she said, and struck a match herself.

Martha was sure she could have found some way to do it, but she went forward on her knees so she could see the fire blaze up.

"Rats," Kit muttered. "It blew out."

She struck another match. It also went out before she got it near the sticks.

She moved around so that her body was between the breeze and the waiting wood.

"This time it'll work," she prophesied.

"It had better," Rosemary said, "or you're going to run out of matches."

But this time the match did burn steadily. Kit held it close to the twigs she had used for kindling. They caught.

"Yay!" Martha cried.

Kit waited. The blaze flared, flickered, and died.

"Oh, for crying out loud, let me do it." Rosemary snatched the matches from her sister.

Kit looked as though she had been slapped.

"Kit was doing okay," Martha said, knowing it was not true.

After three tries, Rosemary did get the fire started.

"It just takes a little know-how," she said smugly.

"Now show us how to fix these dinners," Ellen asked Kit hurriedly.

Kit demonstrated. She made a neat job of them, wrapping up some meat, a few pieces of onion, a handful of potatoes, and a handful of carrots in each one. She made an envelope of the tin foil, lapping the ends over so no juice could escape.

"Let me make my own," Martha said.

"You can't," Kit said. "You have a broken arm."

"I can help. I can do part of it," Martha insisted.

Kit spread out the piece of tin foil ready for her. Martha, using her good hand, scooped up the meat and placed it in the center, and then added the other ingredients. But she had to let Kit do the folding.

Who cares? she told herself. It'll be good.

"I'll put it on the fire," she cried, grabbing her dinner.

But the fire had gone out—and the kindling had vanished, all burned to nothing.

"I might have known," Rosemary said.

"You lit it!" Kit cried, tired of being picked on.

"I'll get some of the wood that's already cut for the fireplace," Ellen said, "or we'll never eat tonight."

"But Ellen, that's not like camp," Martha wailed.

"Too bad," Ellen said, and went for wood.

By the time the fire was finally going, they were far too impatient to let it burn down.

"It should be just coals," Kit said.

"We can put them out of the actual flames," Ellen said, laying her tin-foil envelope at the edge of the blaze. "It'll be okay."

They sat and waited. Martha picked up a long stick and tried to move hers a little closer to direct heat.

"Martha, don't!" Kit cried one second too late. "You'll poke a hole in it and ruin it."

"I didn't. It's fine," Martha said.

But she was pretty sure she had.

Suddenly there was a sizzling sound and a smell began drifting up from the fire. Just a faint smell of onions, but instantly they all realized how ravenous they actually were.

"It's after six," Rosemary said. "And we started before five. Honestly!"

Then she took up Martha's stick and gave her own dinner a nudge.

"I think it's done," she said.

"It'll be raw," Kit told her. "They're just beginning to cook and yours is on the outside edge."

Rosemary hauled her dinner out, using Martha's stick again.

"I'll open it up and see," she said. "I don't want it burned."

206

She unwrapped the dinner with great care, picked up her fork and tried to spear a piece of carrot. The fork would not go into it.

"Kit's right. It isn't cooked," Ellen said. "Wrap it up again."

Rosemary tossed her head. "It's just the way I like it," she retorted.

She tried to get a bite onto her fork. Ellen peered over her shoulder.

"The meat's bleeding," she said. "Here. Let me put it back."

Rosemary gave in, looking sulky. Martha peered at her own package of food. The fire had gone out where it lay. Nothing was happening to it. Nothing at all.

They went on waiting.

"Are you having a great time, Martha?" Rosemary said.

Martha wanted to cry, but she didn't.

"Sure," she said. "It's going to be delicious."

Rosemary looked down at her hands as though she was suddenly ashamed.

"Maybe," she said. "I hope so."

Dinner tasted terrible. The juice had escaped and the bottom of the dinner was burned black. But the vegetables were not all cooked through. Martha bravely munched on one bite and then another. Kit struggled with hers. It was mostly raw. Martha could hear the potatoes crunch. She could see Rosemary's food was as blackened as her own, but she did her best to eat it.

Ellen was the one who balked.

"This is absolutely horrible," she said, dropping her dinner on the sand. "And it would take forever to do it properly. The fire's out again, and we've no more small stuff to light it. All that log of yours is doing, Martha, is getting in the way. Let's go inside and make some soup or something."

Kit looked at Martha.

Rosemary, putting down her dinner almost un-tasted, laughed.

"We sure seem to be great at wrecking meals this week," she said. "I'm for giving up too. I knew all along . . ."

This time, Martha had no fight left in her. She jumped up and ran for the cottage. She did not turn her head when Ellen called after her. She did not stop till she reached her room. Then she slammed the door and dropped onto her bed, sobbing.

Even as she wept, she listened for the others, but nobody followed her. Several minutes passed and she had almost stopped crying when she heard the others coming in.

"We can try it at least . . ." she heard Kit say.

"Maybe it'll go wrong too," Rosemary answered.

Martha really listened, breath held, but someone turned on a tap and then they must have gone into the kitchen for she heard nothing more.

Not that she cared!

Kit opened the door and came in quietly. She had a plate of hot dogs and glasses of milk. Without mentioning the change in menu, she set the tray on the table between their beds where Martha could easily reach.

"Marth, I'm really sorry it didn't work," she said then.

Martha swallowed and faced her.

"Well, you'll be glad to know this settles it," she said, her voice rough. "I'm not at camp and there's no sense pretending I am. Not that it really matters a hoot! Who needs camp?"

Kit did not answer right away. When she did she spoke to Martha's back, for Martha had turned away from her so Kit would not see her struggle not to cry.

"You know," Kit said slowly, "what you need is a bit of your own advice."

Martha, startled, jerked about and stared at her.

"What advice?" she growled.

Kit began to sing softly. "Just stand in the wind and eat peanut brittle. Just stand in the wind and eat peanut brittle."

"You are right out of your mind," Martha said flatly. "Anyway I don't see what that has to do with this."

Kit must have had only a vague idea herself for her words stumbled and halted several times as she thought it out aloud. Martha listened in spite of herself.

"You made me stand in the wind and eat that

candy and you . . . or the candy . . . or just standing up there singing . . . made me stop being afraid of the wind. And you told me to stand up to Rosemary, just as if she were another kind of wind, and I've tried . . ."

"And she's still Rosemary," Martha said, remembering how critical Rosemary had been throughout the tin-foil dinner, how her words had cut when she asked, "Are you having a great time, Martha?"

"Well," Kit said with a grin, "the wind didn't stop blowing either. But I'm not scared of it now and I'm not scared of Rosemary either. Not as scared as I was."

She paused and then went on in a low voice, "What I mean is, you said not to give in! You said to stand up and fight back!"

"I know what I said," Martha told her, "but I'm not scared of anything."

"Not scared exactly," Kit agreed, "but you *are* giving in. You wanted us to be a camp but when things go wrong, you quit."

But what else can I do? Martha cried out inside herself. I tried when we went Orienteering. I tried when we sang by the fire. I tried so hard tonight. But every time something goes wrong, and I just can't try any more.

She wanted to shout the words at Kit and make her say she understood, but she could not. She knew she would burst into tears before she got the first sentence out. Her arm had been jarred when she flung herself down on the bed and now it ached. She had burned her tongue on her tin-foil dinner. And she felt tired right down to her toes with the tiredness of defeat.

Yet she had to say something. Anything to stop the silence after Kit's words.

"There's no peanut brittle," she said, "so it's no use."

Half turned away though she still was, Martha could see Kit smile. Martha wanted to hit her. But what was Kit saying now? Was it the nonsense it sounded or did it mean something?

"If you stop giving up, I promise there'll be peanut brittle."

"What do you mean?" Martha demanded, sitting up straight and giving Kit a suspicious look.

"Never you mind. Try it and see," Kit challenged.

Martha's immense weariness suddenly lifted and hope sprang up in her like a clear fountain. Kit never teased to be mean. Peanut brittle, this time, judging from Kit's voice and her sparkling eyes, was not just candy but something new and different and special. A plan!

"What is it? What are you talking about really?" she demanded.

"Ask me no questions and I'll tell you no lies," Kit evaded, looking suddenly nervous at the abrupt change in Martha. Then she added in a burst,

211

"Only, please, Martha, don't spend time feeling bad. We only have a day and a half left."

"Okay," Martha said. "It was just that . . ."

"I know how it was," Kit replied. "But tonight's a full moon and Ellen says if we stay together in where it's shallow, we can go for a moonlight swim."

"Well, why didn't you say so in the first place?" Martha cried, jumping up to snatch her dry bathing suit down from its hook.

"Because the moon doesn't rise till after dark, dopey," Kit said. "Now finish eating your supper."

I wonder why she bothered with all that stuff about the wind and peanut brittle, Martha thought, her mouth too full of hot dog to ask.

Suddenly Kit, lying back on her bed, laughed aloud. Martha swallowed her bite of hot dog.

"What is so funny all of a sudden?" she asked.

"Nothing," Kit said, looking up at the rafters. Then, using words Martha had spoken before her, she added, "I'm just happy, I guess."

Martha, about to take her last sip of milk, paused and thought about that. Half an hour ago she had felt sure she could never be happy again. Now . . .

"Me too," said Martha in astonishment.

212

18 | Everybody Surprises Martha

The next morning Martha's sleep was shattered by the blast of a whistle. Before she knew who or where she was, she heard Ellen call.

"Rising Whistle for Camp Better-Than-Nothing! All campers report immediately for Morning Dip. And that means you, too, Rosemary Swann!"

Martha sprang out of bed, laughing with delight. Kit sat up and grinned at her.

"This is why you told me not to give up," Martha said, hurrying out of her pajamas.

"Mmmm," Kit said, too busy getting into her bathing suit to answer properly.

They met Ellen in the hall and advanced upon Rosemary, who had not stirred from her bed.

"Ooooh, I have a terrible pain," Rosemary began, before they could open their mouths. "I think I'm dying. Delayed ointment poisoning. Call the camp nurse, somebody!"

"Forget the camp nurse," Ellen said, and Kit darted forward and heartlessly swashed a cold wet washcloth over her sister's face.

"You little wretch!" Rosemary spluttered and was out of bed with a bound, obviously intending to kill

Kit that minute. Ellen blocked her path.

"Here's your bathing suit, camper," she said. "Speed it up. If you aren't down there by the time the rest of us are, you get to wash dishes all day. I'm the Camp Director, so beware!"

The water was like ice, but Rosemary plunged into it at the same moment the others did. They splashed each other and yelled with laughter, forgetting that other cottagers might want to sleep.

Shivering, teeth chattering, they raced back to the cottage and dressed. When they came down to breakfast Martha saw a sheet of paper stuck up on the wall. She read it with wide eyes.

CAMP SCHEDULE

7:30	Morning Dip
8:00	Breakfast
8:30	Dishes (Kit and Ellen) *
9:00	Cabin Cleanup (Inspection will be held)
9:30	Camp Hike to the River's Source (maybe)
11:00	All-Camp Swim
12:00	Dinner
12:30	Dishes (Rosemary and Ellen) *
1:00	Rest Hour
2:00	Camp Activity (to be named by Director)
3:00	Swim
4:00	Free Time
5:00	Supper
5:30	Dishes (Kit and Rosemary) *
Later	Evening Program (planned by Director)
10:00	Lights Out

* *Martha gets to put dishes away after every meal.*

214

"A whole camp day," Martha breathed. For a moment she was so happy she could neither move nor speak. Then as she whirled to face the planners of it, she suddenly wondered if it would really work. She had maintained from the beginning that it would if they would really try it, but thinking back, she was not so sure. Still, so far it had been exactly right.

"Oh, it'll be wonderful," she said. "What a perfect way to spend our last day."

Her own joy ebbed with the words and she saw sadness touch the faces of the others too.

"What's the Evening Program going to be?" she asked. "Tracey says that's the best part of camp."

"You wait and see. Breakfast!" Ellen announced.

When they were seated, she asked if anyone knew a grace to sing the way kids did at camp. Rosemary taught them one. Martha really liked it; it put into words her joy in the day.

> *God has created a new day,*
> *Silver and green and gold.*
> *Live that the sunset may find us*
> *Worthy this gift to hold.*

"You don't seriously believe we'll find the source of the river after all this time," Martha challenged Ellen as they ate.

"No harm in trying. We've never had these two great Orienteerers with us before. It may make all the difference," Ellen said with a grin.

215

The river was merely a lazy creek which came wandering down to the lake through a tangle of brambles and fallen branches, old stumps and rocky treacherous places. The Winston family had set out several times, inspired by Ellen's enthusiasm for Arthur Ransome's heroes and heroines who were forever discovering things and marking them on maps. But the Winstons had always had the two boys along and carried a formidable picnic lunch, so long before they ever arrived, someone was too hungry or too tired or too bitten by bugs and scratched by sharp twigs to go another inch.

"This time we're going to use some brains," Ellen said and insisted, even though it was a warm day, that they wear long-sleeved shirts, blue jeans, thick socks and good hiking shoes. They also sprayed all exposed areas liberally with bug spray and they took nothing to eat.

"Not even candy bars to keep our strength up?" wheedled Martha.

"Eat it before we leave, Marth, if you have to eat. This is your great chance to work off some of that puppy fat with exercise."

"Shut up about puppy fat," Martha warned, but she left her chocolate bar at home.

In spite of their spirit of determination, they were on the point of giving up when they rounded one last boulder and there it was! A small spring, sluggish because it was choked with leaves and bits of bark and mud. They dropped to their knees in a circle around it and even Rosemary made no attempt to hide her excitement as they scooped away with their hands, clearing out the debris. Moments later, their spring—for they felt it was their own—bubbled up bright and clear in the dappled sunlight. They waited in silence, sitting back on their heels, just watching it and listening to the sound it made. Then each in turn leaned forward, cupped her hands and drank the cold, fresh water.

"I'm never going to forget us being here," Martha said as they got up finally to go.

Later, when the four of them went swimming, Martha was happy right down to her toes. It was turning into such a perfect day, better than anything she could have imagined.

Then Rosemary and Ellen went out of the water.

"You two stay in," Ellen instructed. "We have something to do."

Martha and Kit went on splashing about in the water till Kit, as usual, turned blue around her mouth and had to get warm. Teeth chattering, she ran ahead to get into dry clothes, leaving Martha to bring her own towel and the suntan lotion the older girls had forgotten.

Martha, following, sang to herself.

The more we are together, together, together,
The more we are together the campier it gets.

When she entered the cottage, Ellen was talking on the phone. Not really intending to, Martha listened automatically.

"Kit says we really don't need them," Ellen was saying, "so if it's okay with you, we'll get along with what's here."

What on earth was Ellen talking about? Ellen, not seeing Martha behind her, went on, "No, we haven't told her yet. I don't think she suspects a thing. . . ."

At that, she turned, saw Martha and said much too quickly into the phone, "That's all I can say right now. Yes, she is. But thanks a lot. Good-bye, Mother."

"What did Mother call for?" Martha asked, not beating about the bush.

Ellen looked rattled.

"She didn't call. I called her."

"Why?"

"I . . . Well, I . . . What does it matter? Martha, isn't that Kit calling you from outside? You'd better go," Ellen urged.

"It so happens she's upstairs taking off her bathing suit," Martha corrected neatly.

Rosemary, who had been standing by, broke in, "Then it must have been from upstairs we heard her calling. She sounded in a hurry, Martha. You'd better go and investigate."

Martha Jane Winston was not about to move. What were they trying to pull?

218

Then Kit appeared on the stairs. She looked down at them.

"What's happening?" she asked.

Martha noticed that she too had a peculiar note in her voice. Kit was definitely in on it, whatever it was.

"Ellen phoned Mother and she won't tell me why," Martha said.

"Why should she?" Rosemary asked too lightly. "Can't a girl have private things she wants to discuss with her mother?"

"It wasn't like that and you know it," Martha said, anger rising in her against the three of them, plotting and leaving her out.

Then Kit ran down the stairs and grabbed hold of Martha's hand.

"Marth, come on outside with me," she said.

"I just came in. Anyway, why should I?"

Ellen sighed, Rosemary's lips tightened but Kit put her arm right around Martha and spoke with understanding.

"It's something you'll really like, Marth, honest," she said, "but it's a surprise. Now come on and don't spoil it."

Martha stared at her and then at the others. She saw now that they were all smiling at her in a special way. But it was queer being on the outside.

"When do I get to see it?" she demanded, still not moving.

"Tonight. Now don't ask me anything else," Kit begged, "because I'm terrible at keeping secrets and it wouldn't be fair. Just come with me."

Martha took a deep breath, let it go, and then followed Kit back up the stairs. But she did not leave Kit Swann in peace. Oh, no! She hammered her with questions.

"How big is it? Who's bringing it? What does Mother have to do with it? Aw, Kit, come on. Whose idea was it? Is this part of what you were talking about last night, part of my peanut brittle?"

Kit clamped her lips shut and shook her head no matter how Martha pestered.

Martha herself wore down eventually but she made one last try.

"Kit, please, I won't bother you any more if you'll only give me one tiny hint."

"I'm no good at hinting but I'll tell you this much and no more. It *is* part of what I meant last night, maybe the best part. Now quit, Martha. It won't be that long to wait."

"Hours," Martha moaned.

She did get some further clues, though, as the day wore on. When the sky grew hazy, she saw the others looking through the windows with worried eyes. Whatever the secret was, good weather must be important. Martha prayed for sunshine. Then, inspired, she dug out Bruce's wishing stone from one of her pockets in the dirty-clothes hamper. Hoping she was doing it right, she rubbed it and said three

220

times in her most solemn voice, "Let the sun shine! It is my wish."

The sky cleared.

"Rest Hour," Ellen read out the minute the dinner dishes were finished.

"Aw, Ellen, not really," Martha protested, but Ellen was firm and the others backed her up. Every camp had a Rest Hour.

"And if you hear any noises, stay on your beds," Ellen said. "And don't argue, Martha. The Director and her Assistant don't take a Rest Hour every day."

"I can't figure it out," Martha fumed, lying on her bed. Kit had her nose buried in a book.

"Kit, talk to me," Martha demanded.

"You aren't supposed to talk during Rest Hour," Kit whispered, and went on reading, but Martha saw one corner of her mouth quirk up as though she were struggling not to laugh.

"Oh, rats!" Martha muttered. But secretly she was relishing it now. The suspense was awful, but it was fun too, guessing and watching for clues. She listened hard. Ellen and Rosemary were carrying things to the sun porch.

"Here. Let me take part of that," she heard Rosemary say.

The minute Rest Hour was over, Martha planned to raid that sun porch and look over whatever was out there.

But at the end of the hour, Ellen and Rosemary

came running upstairs, and Ellen announced that the next planned activity was reading the rest of *Little Plum*. They had finished *Miss Happiness and Miss Flower* the first night, but were only halfway through the sequel.

"But it's only two o'clock," Martha protested. "We read at night in bed."

"I think we ought to finish it now," Ellen said. "Rosemary and Kit leave tomorrow, you know. We won't finish if we don't do it now. . . . I mean . . . they'll have to pack."

Martha knew it would not take Kit that long to pack. She had been living out of her suitcase all week. Ellen was not making sense.

"Marth, I can't wait till night to find out how it ends," Kit said.

"Me neither," Rosemary chimed in.

That was definitely fishy. Martha knew *Little Plum* was far too young a book for Rosemary to get that excited about.

"Remember, we've never read it before," Kit went on.

Martha did understand that it was hard not to read on when you were worried about the people in a story. She knew everything would be fine, but the others only knew that Nona was miserable because Belinda was fighting with the girl next door.

"Okay," Martha said slowly. Listening, she forgot even the secret they were hiding from her as the story worked out.

When it was finished and she was free to go, Martha ran down the stairs and headed for the sun porch. There was a sheet tacked up over the inside door, and on it a sign reading:

NO CAMPERS ALLOWED PAST THIS SIGN.
SEVERE PENALTIES FOR PEEKING EVEN. THIS
MEANS YOU, MARTHA WINSTON.

THE DIRECTOR.

Martha almost looked anyway, but she managed to stop herself, and, one second later, Kit was there dragging her away to go swimming again.

It was fun in the water. Martha was used to swimming with her sling on now, and she had even picked up some pointers from Kit about how to use her good arm and her legs to better advantage. Also, Kit had finally taught her how to breathe properly when she did the crawl. People had been working on that for ages, but Martha had not mastered it till this week.

Still, even though she kept telling herself to have fun every moment, and not wish time to go any faster, she longed to learn what the big secret was. Waiting was getting to be almost more than she could bear.

Then, wonder of wonders, Kit suggested they play Monopoly. All week Martha had been wanting to play Monopoly but nobody had ever agreed before. All four of them played. Martha, for once, had the luck she had longed for during her many bouts of gin rummy, and she bankrupted the others one by one. It was a glorious game, and it took them till five o'clock to finish.

Then Ellen got supper.

"What's come over you?" Martha asked, amazed.

Ellen never got supper till the last possible minute. A couple of times when they had eaten, it had already been dark out.

"Eat, child," Ellen ordered. "I have my reasons."

Martha ate, but she hardly tasted the food. Surely the time must be almost up!

"Okay," Ellen said grinning. "We might as well tell her now."

"If you don't," Martha threatened, "I'm going to burst."

"It was Kit's idea," Ellen said, maddeningly still not explaining a thing.

"ELLEN, TELL ME!" shrieked her sister.

Kit giggled and told.

"We're going on a real camp sleep-out," she said. "We'll sleep under the stars just like you said. And we'll have a campfire and sing. Martha, are you pleased?"

Martha for once in her life was speechless.

"Marth, say something!" Kit begged.

"Oh," Martha breathed. "Oh Ellen, oh Kit!"

"How about 'Oh Rosemary!'" Rosemary asked, laughing.

"Oh Rosemary!" Martha said obediently.

Then she leaped to her feet and stared around from one to the other of them.

"It'll be perfect. I know it will be perfect," she declared.

"If it doesn't rain," said Ellen. "With our luck, something is sure to go wrong."

"But Mother took my sleeping bag back to town," Martha remembered, ignoring Ellen.

Rosemary groaned.

"You won't believe this," she said to Martha, "but Kit, the camping expert, declares we don't need sleeping bags, let alone air mattresses."

"I keep telling you I really and truly do know how to make a bedroll." Kit stuck up for herself. "You'll see."

"Well, the closer I get to that bedroll, the more comfortable my real bed looks," Rosemary said.

Ellen laughed at her.

"I'd like to see what you'd do if we went off and left you behind," she said.

"Okay, I admit it," Rosemary said, getting to her feet. "Let's get started."

Ellen issued instructions like a drill sergeant. Already Rosemary and Ellen had piled most of the things they were going to take on the sun-porch floor. Now Kit and Martha added their bedding.

"It's a good thing we're only going to that stand of pines," Ellen said, looking across the back road at the tall trees. "We'd never make it if we had to lug this stuff far."

They loaded Rosemary down first. Pillows bulged under her elbows and her arms were strained around an awkward bundle of blankets. Ellen took the rest of the bedding and a mysterious paper bag which she would not let Martha see into.

"It's the provision bag," she said.

Kit had mosquito stuff and a package of vanilla wafers which Martha insisted they take in case Ellen's provisions gave out. She also toted a bulky tarpaulin. Martha, with only one carrying arm, brought oranges and her flashlight with the brand-new batteries. She could hardly wait till it grew dark enough to use it.

"I won't need my plastic soap dish, will I?" she asked Ellen.

"There's no water over there," Ellen told her. "Besides, you ought to save something for next year."

"Let's go!" Rosemary cried. "My arms are breaking."

Nobody had a free hand to open the back door. Martha, giggling, put down the things she was carrying and held it wide. Ellen glanced back at the other two pillows, a box of paper, and half a dozen logs for the fire, the matches and some plastic garbage bags she was taking along to keep the dew off.

"We'll have to make another trip," she said.

226

It was nearly sunset by the time they had everything at their campsite.

Ellen and Martha set out on a search for small twigs and sticks to help get the fire started. Under the trees, there were lots to choose from.

"We should have come here last night," Ellen said.

"That's for sure," Martha agreed, but no shadow came from the evening before to dim her present joy.

Kit began sorting things out so they would know where to start. When Martha and Ellen arrived with hands full of kindling, Rosemary built the fire.

"I hope it goes," Kit murmured.

"Don't worry," Rosemary said. "I know what I'm doing."

"You'd better get the beds made, Kit, before we light the fire," Ellen said. "Otherwise you'll be falling over yourself in the dark."

"Right away," Kit said and began. Martha watched her with awe. Kit seemed to have no hesitation whatever. She folded corners in and tucked edges under until each bed was like a long narrow envelope with an opening at one end. When hers was done, Martha went over to look at it more closely.

"Hey, Kit," she said uneasily. "I think I'm wider than this bed."

"Don't worry," Kit told her. "I'll adjust it."

Then it really was time for the fire. It blazed up magnificently, making a satisfying crackling noise as the wood caught. The four of them sat around it. The three who had been campers sang,

> *Fire's burning. Fire's burning.*
> *Draw nearer. Draw nearer.*
> *In the gloaming, in the gloaming,*
> *Come sing and be merry.*

They sang it over again until Martha was sure of the words, and then they sang it in a round. Kit, who had trouble holding to her own tune, sang with her hands over her ears.

They sang other songs after that, including their national anthems.

"They aren't exactly camp songs," Ellen said, "but we learned them at this camp."

"Let's sing one more, and then the fire will be about right for cooking," Kit said mysteriously.

Martha, much as she loved food, felt anxious. They had not had good luck with cooking before.

Don't let it spoil things, she wished.

"I know another round that's really pretty," Rosemary told them. She taught them "Shalom, Chaverim."

"What do the words mean?" Martha asked.

It had sounded so lovely and haunting as their voices blended in the clear evening air.

"There's a translation in the book," Rosemary said. She sounded shy.

"Well, tell us," Ellen said.

228

"No. Sing it, Rosemary," Kit ordered.

Farewell, good friends, farewell, good friends,
Farewell, farewell.
Till we meet again, till we meet again,
Farewell, farewell.

Nobody said anything for a moment after she finished. Martha felt as though she was going to cry.
They were going away tomorrow, Rosemary and
Kit. Who would she feed the gulls with? Who would
she talk to in bed at night? Ellen was a good sister,
but she usually came to bed after Martha was asleep.

In the darkness she felt for Kit's hand. Kit's fingers met hers and linked with them.

"Provision time!" Ellen said suddenly, breaking
the spell. "Let's eat."

Then Kit dove into the bag and came up with
marshmallows, peanut butter, graham wafers and
chocolate bars. Martha stared.

"We're going to make S'mores," Kit told her.
"They're easy. First you get your graham crackers
all ready."

She laid out two graham crackers and put some
squares of chocolate on one, peanut butter on the
other. Then she proceeded to toast a marshmallow.
As Martha already knew, Kit was a patient roaster
of marshmallows. It was finally done, golden brown
on all sides.

Martha's mouth was watering. Kit put the marsh-mallow on top of the chocolate and laid the graham cracker on top.

"Then you just squish it," she said and did.

She handed it to Martha. "Go ahead," she said. "Try it."

Martha thought it was wonderful. Rosemary said they were too sweet but she went right ahead and made another. The chocolate partly melted and combined with the marshmallow and peanut butter. Martha understood why the whole thing was called "S'more."

"I want some more too," she said. "And I can do it myself." It took her longer and her marshmallow was a bit charred, but it was scrumptious.

When they had finished, Ellen pulled out her whistle and was about to blow Lights Out.

"We didn't sing 'Taps,' " Kit objected.

So they stood up, crossed their hands, right over left, making a circle, and sang,

Day is done.
Gone the sun
From the lakes,
From the hills,
From the sky.
All is well.
Safely rest.
God is nigh.

231

Martha turned away from the fire and looked into the darkness.

"Where's my bed?" she said.

"Now's your chance," Ellen said quickly. "Where's that flashlight with the brand-new batteries?"

Martha had to laugh.

"I left it in my bed," she confessed.

"Here, Marth," Kit called. "You're right next to me."

And the flashlight beam, shining from Kit's hand instead of her own, guided her to her bedroll.

19 | It's a Secret

"When you take your shoes off, put them down inside your bed so they'll keep dry," Kit said.

Martha was not worried about her sneakers getting wet, but she grabbed the package of vanilla wafers and pushed it down under the covers. Then, with care, she inserted herself into her strange bed. There was a hard lump under her in the sand. She bent so she would go around it. Suddenly her right foot poked through the neat end of her blankets. She pulled it back hastily and then tried to get her arm, in its sling, to fit in comfortably. The sides were coming untucked.

Martha lay still and did not say anything. Let Kit believe she really did know how.

"Heavens," said Kit beside her. "I'll have to get back out and tuck myself in."

"Tuck me in while you're up," Rosemary said.

"And me," Ellen and Martha said together.

Giggling, Kit went from bed to bed. When she was finished, Martha felt snug. Then Kit slid back into her own bed, and the four of them lay still. Ellen and Rosemary started to talk quietly. They were on the far side of the fire. Martha turned her head so that she faced Kit.

"You know what?" she said softly. "I don't even notice your accent any longer."

Kit's head popped up.

"MY accent!" she exclaimed. "What do you mean —*my* accent?"

"Didn't you know you have an American accent?" Martha asked, as startled as Kit.

"You mean YOU have a Canadian accent," Kit countered. "You should hear the way you say 'about' and 'house.'"

"But you say 'abowwt,'" Martha objected. "And you say 'pour' when you mean 'poor.'"

Suddenly they were both laughing.

"I didn't know I had an accent," Kit said. She thought about it and then added, "I never really felt especially American until I came up here."

"Well, I still can't hear any accent when I talk," Martha said, listening to herself. "But I feel more Canadian too. I feel as though I've traveled."

"Dope, I'm the one who traveled," Kit said.

Yet Martha still felt she had been somewhere. The world seemed bigger than it had been.

She lay there thinking about it, and then, all at once, she saw a familiar pattern in the stars.

"Look! There's the Big Dipper!" she cried.

"I don't see it," Kit said. "I always have trouble finding it and when I do, it never looks like a dipper to me."

Martha reached into her sleeping bag and pulled out her flashlight. She was going to get to use it after all.

"Watch. I'll show you," she said, and traced the tilted Dipper with the line of light.

"I see it," Kit said. "I see it, Marth."

Her voice shook.

"What's the matter?" Martha asked.

"Nothing," Kit said. "It's just that tomorrow . . . Well, I've had a great time, that's all. Feeding the gulls and saving that bat and . . ."

Her voice faltered. Martha, not wanting to cry, laughed instead.

"And eating those delicious pork chops," she teased. "And going Orienteering with Toby and making those absolutely yummy tin-foil dinners!"

"I never thought you'd laugh about that," Kit said.

"Me neither," Martha admitted, "but it seems funny now."

"You two, go to sleep," Ellen called softly across to them.

"Okay," Martha called back.

"Night, Marth," Kit said.

"Good night."

Then Martha just lay there, looking up at the frosty light of the stars, the huge dark sky, the black shadows of the trees. She was sleeping out!

When she wakened, an hour or two later, the other three were sound asleep.

"Kit," she whispered.

Kit, curled up beside her, did not stir.

Martha lay wondering why she had wakened. Then she saw a slow tide of silver washing over the trees. She put her good arm out and crooked it under her head. The stars, so bright when she and Kit were talking, paled as she watched. Then she saw the white edge come up over the sand hills, and the moon rose.

"Kit," Martha tried again, wanting to share it.

But Kit slept on. Slowly the moon sailed up the sky. As it snagged in the bottom branches of a pine, Martha gave a long sigh at the beauty of it and went back to sleep herself.

It was just after dawn when Ellen called her.

"Martha! Martha! Wake UP!"

Before she opened her eyes, she knew why Ellen was sounding frantic. It was raining.

"Rats!" Martha said, and struggled out of her cocoon of blankets.

Kit was rubbing her eyes. Rosemary, her arms full of bedding, was already headed for the cottage.

Snatching up her pillow, Martha raced after Rosemary. What a time to have a broken arm! She dumped her load and started to follow Rosemary back out into the rain.

"Hold the door," Ellen called. "It'll be more help than you trying to lug stuff."

Here came Kit, her bedroll draped over her head. One more trip for all three of them, and everything was in the cottage. They stood in the sun porch and looked at each other.

"No matter what we do, no matter how hard we try, something goes wrong," Ellen lamented.

But this time, Martha felt no despair. Not even disappointment.

"It's more exciting this way," she declared. "And it's morning anyway, so what does it matter?"

"I'm cold," Kit said.

"No wonder. You're soaked." Rosemary shooed her sister up the stairs. Ellen and Martha followed.

"I'll make cocoa," Ellen said as she went to get into dry clothes.

The cocoa turned out to be exactly right. Kit, lowering her steaming mug, gave Martha a sudden smile.

"We have hot chocolate at camp almost every morning, Marth," she said.

Martha beamed. What did it matter that they had been drenched? Her flashlight still worked perfectly, and they had actually had a camp sleep-out.

She had always known camp would be like this—friends laughing together and planning special things to do.

Long ago, before the Swanns came, Ellen had asked her, "What's so special about camp?" And she had not known the answer.

But now she thought she did. It was a new kind of friendship. Not just two people, but a group. Four, six, or seventy—what did it matter? It was a group that laughed at the same jokes, suffered the same setbacks, shared the same moments of triumph, and cared about each other and lived each moment enjoying it more because they were together. Until they became one with each other. The oneness—that was what was special.

"What'll we do next?" she asked happily.

Ellen stared at her. Her answer hit Martha like a slap in the face.

"We'll hang up everything to dry. Then we'll get ready for the Swanns' coming," she said. "They should be here before lunch. Mother said they planned to make an early start on their trip home."

"But . . ." Martha started and did not know how to finish. There was no arguing her way around it. Camp Better-Than-Nothing was finishing. Just when it had properly begun.

From that moment, Martha fought to hold the day back, to make each moment last. The others did too. When the bedding was draped here and there around the cottage to dry, Ellen gave in to Martha's pleading to play one final game of gin rummy.

"Although the house is filthy," she said.

Rosemary won.

"About time!" she announced, giving Kit a dark look.

"Let's keep on playing till Kit wins," Martha begged. "She really ought to win the last game."

"There just isn't time," Ellen said, putting the cards back in the box.

"Besides, I have to be generous and let other people win sometimes," Kit said with a real Martha grin.

The younger girls swam while the older two cleaned. The rain had blown away as quickly as it had come. It was a perfect day.

A perfect day for nothing! Martha thought.

Later when the two of them were getting dressed, Kit looked down at her bare legs and laughed.

"This week has made a wreck out of me," she declared. "Look at the five thousand mosquito bites I got Orienteering, and scratches, too, from when we galloped off with the money bags. I went right through a bush. And I burned my hand on the frying pan when I was making pancakes. It's not so bad, but you can still see the place."

"That's not all," Martha said. "You haven't combed your hair for three days and you're really brown."

"It isn't dirt," Kit said.

"How do you know?" Martha asked. "You haven't tried washing it off."

"I've been swimming nearly every day," Kit said. She looked down at her grubby shorts and crumpled shirt. "Maybe I ought to put on something else though," she added uneasily, "before Mother comes."

"You look okay," Martha told her. "Besides, you haven't anything else clean, have you?"

"I have the dress I came in," Kit said. "But I think it's too wrinkled to wear. I put it under everything else in the suitcase."

"Zip me up at the back, will you, please?" Martha asked.

Kit went behind her, but she did not do up the zipper right away. Instead she blurted, "Marth, thanks a lot for everything. I mean, I think Rosemary and I will have a lot more fun together now. We're still different and everything, but I feel more like her sister, and she does too. Something like you and Ellen. And . . . my report card always says I'm 'Withdrawn,' but nobody could stay withdrawn with a friend like you around. Anyway, that's what I wanted to say. Sort of," she finished helplessly.

Martha wanted to whirl around and hug her, but instead she joked. "Christine used to be withdrawn but an excellent student. Now she is the most popular girl in the school, but she is failing in all sub-

jects. Could you please urge her to go back to being withdrawn?"

Kit laughed shakily. Martha took a deep breath. What could she say? That this week had been the best week in her life in spite of all the bad times? That Kit wasn't just one of her many friends, but somebody special—and not a bit like a mouse any longer?

"I . . ." she started in and hesitated.

"Kit! Martha! They're here! Come on down!" Ellen called.

"I never did do up your zipper," Kit said, and moved to fix it.

The next moment Mrs. Swann was standing in the doorway.

"Hello, Martha dear," she said. "Christine, sweetheart, you can't go anywhere looking like that! I've some clean clothes for you in the car. Take those things off while I fetch them. And wash! Martha, your mother wants you."

"I look okay," Martha heard Kit say, but Mrs. Swann paid no attention. She swept Martha out of the room with her, and from then on, for Martha, a strange nightmare took over the morning.

She could not seem to get near Kit.

When she had reported to her mother and agreed to get her things moved back in with Ellen, she ran back up the stairs. Kit, scrubbed within an inch of her life, was sitting very straight on the

242

one chair in the bedroom. She had on her white sandals, lemon-yellow slacks and a crisp white top. Mrs. Swann was hard at work combing the tangles out of her hair.

"Mother, I can comb my own hair," Kit was saying. "I've done it for myself all week."

"Yes, and it looks it," Mrs. Swann answered, still combing. She made a part in Kit's hair as straight as a ruler.

"Now, let me look at those fingernails," Mrs. Swann said.

And Martha, watching, saw the fight go out of Kit. The Kit Martha knew and loved seemed to vanish without a trace, and baby Christine was there in her place, meekly holding out her hand.

Martha fled.

Half an hour later, Caroline Winston sent her up to check and see if anything had been left behind.

"And look properly, Martha. Under the beds and behind things."

"Okay, okay," Martha growled.

Kit's raincoat still hung on a hook behind the bedroom door. Martha took it down and started to leave the room. Then, remembering her Mother's instructions, she turned back for another look. There was an envelope lying on top of her pillow. It had her name written on it in Kit's writing.

Martha tore it open. Inside was Kit's dollar and seventy-five cents and a note.

Dear Marth,
   This is for bread for the gulls.
Say Hi to them for me.
I have to go.
         Love,
         Kit
         A Rich American.

I should give her something, Martha thought.
Something special. Something to help her stay brave.

Then, inspired, she dumped the coat on her bed,
yanked out her shoe box of tricks and looked in it
for something to send home with Kit.

If she really has nerve enough to use it, Martha
said to herself.

There were lots of things. Choosing was hard.
And she only had a second. Her hand hovered over
fake bandages, a plastic eye to drop in someone's
water glass, a spoon that bent when you tried to eat
with it. Then quickly, before she could weaken, she
grabbed her favorite, Henrietta, and slid her into
the raincoat pocket. She ran down the stairs.

"Here," she said to Christine Swann, standing
silently at her mother's side. "You forgot your coat."

"Oh. Thank you," Kit said.

Martha bit her lip. She would not cry. Not with
that fancy Mrs. Swann watching.

Then everyone began moving to the car. Rosemary actually leaned over and hugged Martha be-

fore she climbed into the back seat. Martha tensed. Maybe Kit, too, would do something special at the end.

But she already did do it, a voice inside Martha reminded her. When she told me about making friends. I'm the one who did not say anything.

"Thank you for inviting me," Kit said to Mrs. Winston. "I had a lovely time."

She sounded as though she had been to a birthday party.

"Christine baby, come on," Mrs. Swann urged from inside the car.

"Mother, she's no baby, so stop saying that. It's an insult," Rosemary said from the back seat. She looked at Kit, who was coming towards her. "Don't worry, Kit," she said softly. "We'll be back."

Rosemary Swann, you are a neat sister, Martha thought, and the trance which had held her helpless began to break.

But Kit was in the car now and the door slammed shut between them.

"Good-bye. God bless," Nell Swann said, turning down her window for a final wave. Rosemary's sharp words did not seem to have bothered her.

Mr. Swann and Dad shook hands through the car window on his side.

"Come again any time," Martha heard her father say. "After these few days, Caroline's like a new person."

A new person! Changed! Kit had been that when the two of them had stood together facing the wind and singing like crazy. Kit could not really have become a baby again. Oh, maybe for a minute or two. But not really.

Mr. Swann started the car.

Suddenly Martha saw the back window on her side roll down. Kit was staring out hungrily at everything—the cottage, the golden sand, a slit of blue water glimpsed between the houses, the miraculous blue of their sky, a gull coasting by hoping for a handout. . . .

But she's really looking for me!

With that, Martha had the words she needed, words that Kit, and only Kit, would understand.

The big car had edged out into the lane behind the row of cottages. It was starting to gather speed. Paying no attention to her family, Martha ran after it.

"Kit!" she shouted.

The car kept going. Martha's arm jolted, her side hurt and she was rapidly falling behind. Another minute and there would be no hope of Kit hearing.

"Kit!" Martha screamed, nearly deafening herself. "Don't forget. Stand in the wind . . ."

Her breath gave out. The car was really moving now. She had missed her chance.

Then the answering shout came. Martha saw

246

Kit hanging out the window. Her hair was blowing wildly but she was not caring.

". . . and eat peanut brittle! I remember, Martha," Kit called back.

The car turned the corner and disappeared. Martha, her sling crooked, her grin wide, walked back to her waiting family.

"What on earth was that all about?" her father asked.

"It's a secret," Martha said. "A secret between me and Kit."

"Was it a sort of password?" Bruce asked, his eyes wide.

"Sort of," Martha told him.

"But what does it let you into?" Toby asked.

Martha hesitated. It let them into laughter and sharing and being friends and not minding storms. And a day at Camp Better-Than-Nothing. But she could not explain. She barely understood herself.

"That's a secret too," she said.

Format by Gloria Bressler
Set in 12 pt. Baskerville
Composed by American Book–Stratford Press
Printed by The Murray Printing Co.
Bound by American Book–Stratford Press
HARPER & ROW, PUBLISHERS, INCORPORATED